Horse thief!

"Glory! Oh, Glory, you're here," Cindy breathed with relief. "But how on earth did you get here? And do your owners know you're gone?"

In spite of her delight at finding the colt, Cindy knew she had to act fast. Glory's owners would no doubt be on the lookout for him soon. There was no question in her mind about returning him to them, but what could she do with him? Where could she put him? The obvious answer was to take him to Whitebrook, but if she did that, she knew that Mike and Mr. McLean would have no choice but to contact the owners. Then Cindy remembered something. There was a small storage shed to the rear of the paddocks. She could hide Glory there while she figured out what to do. For an instant, Cindy thought about the consequences of hiding the gray colt. But then she remembered the night she had run away from her old foster parents, ending up asleep in a stall at Whitebrook. Her decision was made. She couldn't let Glory down.

THOROUGHBRED

CINDY'S RUNAWAY COLT

JOANNA CAMPBELL

HarperPaperbacks

A Division of HarperCollins*Publishers*

HarperPaperbacks   *A Division of* HarperCollins*Publishers*
             10 East 53rd Street, New York, N.Y. 10022

Copyright © 1995 by Daniel Weiss Associates, Inc., and Joanna Campbell
Cover art copyright © 1995 Daniel Weiss Associates, Inc.

First printing: May 1995

Printed in the United States of America

HarperPaperbacks and colophon are trademarks of HarperCollins*Publishers*

❖ 10 9 8 7 6 5 4 3 2

CINDY BLAKE CLOSED HER EYES AND BREATHED DEEPLY, inhaling the wonderful smells of Whitebrook Farm: freshly mown grass, polished leather, and, best of all, horses. She was almost afraid to look around, afraid that Whitebrook might have vanished overnight—and her new life along with it. Silently she counted to ten and then opened her eyes again. What she saw made her grin with delight. She didn't think she would ever get used to the sight of the neat, white farmhouse and cottages, the rolling hills, the three low barns, and the fenced paddocks in back where gleaming horses grazed contentedly. In all of her eleven years she hadn't been this happy.

"There's no place like home, is there?" a voice behind her asked gently.

Cindy turned to meet the warm gaze of Samantha McLean. They had just returned from several weeks at Saratoga Racecourse in upstate New York. Cindy had had a fabulous time, but it was wonderful to be back at Whitebrook again.

"There sure isn't," Cindy agreed.

"Well, let's get the horses unloaded," Samantha said with a smile. "They'll be glad to be home, too."

They both turned toward the big six horse van that Mike Reese had parked in the stable yard. Mike and his father were the co-owners of Whitebrook. Mr. Reese had stayed behind to oversee the farm while Mike and his wife, Ashleigh Griffen, Cindy, Samantha, Samantha's stepmother, Beth, and her father, Ian, the head trainer at Whitebrook, had all gone to Saratoga.

In the short time that Cindy had lived on the farm with the McLeans, she had already begun to feel a part of it. It was hard to believe that just a few months before, she had been an orphan on the run with no family or friends to turn to.

Cindy remembered too well that night when, in lonely desperation, she had run away from her latest foster home. Exhausted and sick with fear and hunger, she had taken refuge in the broodmare barn at Whitebrook, curling up in the straw in one of the stalls with two little foals. Samantha had found her there, but instead of being angry and throwing Cindy out, Samantha had brought her to the cottage she shared with her father, given her food and a warm bed. Now Samantha's father and stepmother were Cindy's new foster parents. It seemed too good to be true. She was happier than she had ever been in her life, but she could never forget that she was still a foster child. The Kentucky Child Welfare authorities had the ultimate say about where Cindy would remain. The thought of being forced to leave this wonderful place and these wonderful people sent a shiver down her spine, despite the warm Kentucky afternoon. She quickly shook the thought away.

Mike and Ian McLean were sliding open the side doors of the big van and lowering the ramp. Cindy could hear the snorts and stomping feet of the six horses within. Samantha hurried up the ramp of the van and moments later led out a beautiful roan filly, her own race mare, Shining.

Cindy hurried over to hold Shining while Samantha went back into the van to help with the other horses. Cindy lovingly patted the filly, who had been incredibly successful at Saratoga. She'd won the Grade 1 Alabama Stakes, beating her arch rival, Her Majesty, another three-year-old filly owned by Lavinia Townsend of nearby Townsend Acres. Lavinia, who never had a kind word to say about

Whitebrook, and in particular, Ashleigh, had been ridiculously angry about her horse's loss.

Cindy started walking Shining in a circle to loosen the kinks in her muscles after the long journey. Mike led out his four-year-old sprinter, Blues King, who had delighted them all when he'd won the Forego Handicap two weeks earlier at Saratoga. All in all, it had been a very successful meet for Whitebrook. Two of Mike's less talented horses had won allowance races. The two two-year-olds he'd brought had put in good efforts, and Townsend Princess, the two-year-old filly Ashleigh co-owned with Clay Townsend, owner of Townsend Acres, had won her maiden race by an unbelievable ten lengths. The filly's future looked bright, which it hadn't earlier that year when she had been laid up with a fractured foreleg—an injury caused by Lavinia Townsend's inexperience when she'd ridden Princess in a workout without permission. Because of that incident and countless others, going back to when Ashleigh and Brad Townsend were children, animosity between the two stables lingered.

Unfortunately, Princess was stabled at Townsend Acres and was being trained by the head trainer there, Ken Maddock.

Ashleigh walked over to Cindy as Ian McLean, Len, Whitebrook's stable manager, and Vic, their fulltime groom, led the remaining horses from the van.

"So how's the fastest three-year-old filly at Saratoga?" Ashleigh asked as she smilingly rubbed Shining's ears. "You're sure proving you're Wonder's sister."

Samantha joined them. "She definitely is," she agreed happily. "And when I think what a sorry sight she was shen Mike brought her home from that auction, it almost seems like a miracle."

"A miracle that you helped create," Ashleigh said.

Samantha had told Cindy all the details of Shining's past. The filly, who in her first years, had gone through a succession of owners, ending up in the stables of a third-rate trainer, was half sister to Ashleigh's champion mare, Ashleigh's Wonder. Wonder was now a broodmare at Whitebrook, but during her racing days, had won the Kentucky Derby and the Breeder's Cup Classic. She was just as much of a success as a broodmare and had produced several talented offspring, including Wonder's Pride, who, the previous January, had been named Horse of the Year, Townsend Princess, and the promising yearling, Mr. Wonderful, who would soon begin his yearling training.

"Time to get you in your stall, pretty lady," Samantha said. "Tomorrow, I thought we could go

5

out for a ride," she added to Cindy. "Shining would love to get out on the trails again, and you can ride Bo Jangles."

Cindy didn't need to be asked twice. Ever since Samantha had started teaching her to ride two months before, she'd looked forward to every minute she could spend in the saddle. Samantha had told her she was learning fast and had a natural seat, and nothing could have pleased Cindy more.

Ashleigh headed off to Mike and Ian McLean's office as Samantha and Cindy led Shining into the barn.

"I just hope our girl can keep up her winning streak," Samantha said, gazing at Shining like a proud parent.

"I know she can!" Cindy said loyally.

Samantha smiled at Cindy's confidence. "This month's rest will do her a lot of good. She needs it after Saratoga. We'll see how she feels in October."

They led Shining past a dozen stalls housing gorgeous Thoroughbreds, all of which were in active training.

"Why don't you start grooming her while I get her feed," Samantha said when they reached Shining's stall.

"Sure," Cindy said, walking Shining into the fresh smelling stall. Shining gave a happy wicker, letting them know she was happy to be home. Cindy went back in the aisle to collect a curry comb and some brushes.

Of all the horses in the barn, Cindy felt the tightest bond with Shining. They both had known hardship and unhappiness. Samantha had shown Cindy a picture of Shining when she had first arrived at Whitebrook. The love and care the filly had received since then had made such a difference that Cindy had hardly been able to recognize the thin, mangy, listless horse in the picture.

She swept the soft body brush over the red and white flecked coat. "No one's ever going to neglect you like that again, Shining," she whispered. "You've got a real family now."

With that, Cindy flung her arms around the filly's neck. The thought of Shining's past life had brought a lump to her throat. She, too, knew what it was like to be unloved, trusting no one. If only her own future at Whitebrook was as secure as Shining's.

Cindy felt like she was living a dream. Until now, real life for her had meant not having a family and a home like Whitebrook and a horse to ride. Real life had meant foster parents shouting at her, making her do countless chores. It had meant running away and being totally alone in the world.

Now she was surrounded by warm and loving

people. She was spending each day doing things she enjoyed and learning to ride and care for the horses. And tomorrow she would go riding again with Samantha over the grassy lanes between the paddocks. Cindy smiled as she visualized the two of them trotting their horses over the emerald grass— she would sit proudly in the saddle with her head up, back straight, heels down, and hands easy on the reins, just as Samantha had taught her. Then the two of them would urge their horses into a canter under the bright blue early September sky, feel the bunching of the horses' muscles, the wind on their cheeks.

Cindy sighed and rested her forehead against Shining's sleek neck. It really was a dream come true—but like a dream, Cindy reminded herself that it could end.

As the first day of school approached, Cindy rode almost every day, sometimes asking Samantha or Len to coach her on her seat. Occasionally she even got pointers from Ashleigh. At first, Cindy had been too in awe of the beautiful jockey to ask her for help. But Ashleigh was so nice and friendly and such a patient teacher that she soon put Cindy at ease.

Cindy even found herself confiding to Ashleigh her nervousness about starting sixth grade at a new school. The idea of school had been bothering Cindy from the minute she found out that she was going to be staying at Whitebrook for the fall. Of course, it was nothing like the fear of being taken away or abandoned, but it nagged at her nevertheless.

"I wasn't much for school, either," Ashleigh admitted. "I used to hate to have to leave the horses here. My grades depended on what was happening at the farm. If everything was going well, I did fine. But if there was a sick foal or an important race coming up, forget it! My parents practically had to chain me to the desk."

Cindy chewed her lip nervously. It wasn't exactly grades she was worried about. She usually managed all right with her classes. It was the people Cindy was more afraid of. She had been shuffled around so much that she didn't make friends easily. There just didn't seem to be much point when she never knew if she would be with them again the next year. She felt awkward and embarrassed when she had to explain that she was a foster child, so she tended to keep to herself. "I just wish I knew someone, anyone," she murmured.

Ashleigh smiled warmly. "Is that what you're worried about?"

Cindy nodded glumly.

"Well, I, for one, am *sure* you'll make friends,

Cindy," Ashleigh told her. "It won't be as bad as you think. If you're nervous, just remember how many friends you have here and how many people care about you—not to mention how many horses, cats, and dogs," she added kiddingly.

Cindy grinned. Even at Whitebrook, where the whole staff were animal lovers, she had gotten a reputation for being good with animals. Something about her orphaned past seemed to help her understand them and communicate with them better than the average person. "You're right," she said determinedly, "maybe it won't be that bad."

2

CINDY TRIED TO REMEMBER HER RESOLVE THE NEXT DAY when the bus picked her up at the end of the Whitebrook driveway. Samantha gave her the thumbs up sign from aboard Shining. The older girl's days of "freedom" were over, too: having graduated from Henry Clay High School the previous spring, she had just started classes at the Lexington campus of the University of Kentucky. The only difference was that Samantha had arranged to have mostly late classes so that she could exercise her mounts in the morning. That, Cindy thought wistfully, and the fact that she had friends at the University. Her boyfriend Tor Nelson was a junior, and her best friend Yvonne Ortez was starting her freshman year as well.

The bus was packed by the time Cindy boarded.

She walked quickly to the back to find an empty space, ignoring the curious eyes staring after her. *At least I'm dressed all right,* Cindy told herself, glancing down at her khaki pants and navy polo shirt. She made a mental note to thank Beth again for taking her to the Lexington Mall and buying her new fall clothes. It was just another example of everything the McLeans had done to make her feel at home. At first Cindy had rebuffed all of their efforts to include her; now she was afraid to admit how happy she felt as a member of Whitebrook's extended family. She knew she had let her guard down with the McLeans. She had let herself learn to love them and her surroundings, for better or worse.

Cindy plopped into the first empty seat she came to and didn't look up again until the bus was underway. When she did, she saw that she was surrounded by girls and boys chattering happily about their summers. Every so often, a group would erupt in boisterous laughter. Cindy sank a little lower in her seat. Would any of them be her friends? she wondered. It was one thing to have a loving, new foster family. Having a new friend seemed like more than she could hope for.

By mid-morning, Cindy was completely exhausted. She had run from classroom to classroom, half the time getting lost on the way and showing up late. The teachers were mostly friendly, but by her fourth period French class, Cindy still hadn't met any of the other students. Taking a peek at her schedule, she noted that she had been placed in an intermediate French class. She couldn't understand a word the teacher was saying, so she just stared at the board and tried to look interested.

Evidently the girl in front of her felt the same way. A few minutes into class Cindy noticed she stopped taking notes and started doodling in her notebook. The girl was an incredible artist and, what was more, Cindy saw with delight, she was drawing pictures of horses. As Cindy craned her neck to watch, the girl drew horse after horse—mares and foals grazing, jumpers going over fences, race horses galloping.

Cindy was so caught up in the pictures that she hardly heard the French teacher excuse them for lunch. She hung back in her seat, waiting to see who the girl's friends were. To her surprise, the artist quickly packed up her notebook and books and headed toward the cafeteria alone, her eyes shyly averted downward.

"Hey! Wait a minute!" Cindy called, forgetting her own reserve for the first time that day.

The girl stopped in the hallway and turned uncertainly. She was so pale she that she was almost white. Her hair was a few shades lighter than Cindy's honey blond, and it hung in careless wisps about her face. Cindy ran to catch up with her. "I just wanted to tell you what a great artist you are. I was sitting behind you in French class just now, and I saw the horses you drew."

The girl smiled awkwardly, blushing at the compliment. "Thanks. I love horses," she said quietly. Then she turned and slunk away like a shy animal.

Seeing someone even more reserved than she was instantly gave Cindy courage. "Wait, don't go— maybe we could eat lunch together," she suggested boldly. The girl pursed her lips uncertainly. In an effort to stop her from going, Cindy blurted out, "I'm Cindy, and I love horses, too."

"You do?" the girl asked, stopping short. She flashed Cindy the briefest of smiles, then added, "I'm Heather."

"So you want to have lunch with me, Heather?" Cindy asked.

Heather nodded and waited for Cindy to catch up with her.

The two girls found an empty table in the cafeteria and sat down. The first few minutes were awkward, but then they began to talk. Cindy brought up the girl's drawings again. It turned out that Heather was learning how to ride, but slowly, since she had to borrow a neighbor's horse in exchange for cleaning tack. "There are six kids in my family, and my parents just can't afford a horse," she explained quietly. "It doesn't help that my dad was laid off for almost four months. We moved to Kentucky because he found a job here, but he just started. So things are kind of tight for us right now. But I wish more than anything I could have my own horse," she added with a sigh.

Cindy nodded sympathetically. She understood desperately wanting something and not being able to have it. Hesitantly she described Whitebrook to Heather. She didn't want to seem like she was showing off, but she didn't really think of it as hers, anyway. Heather listened with rapt attention as Cindy named the illustrious horses and told her about Shining and going to Saratoga.

"Wow, are you lucky," Heather breathed.

Cindy shook her head. "Not really," she said, suddenly feeling embarrassed.

"But why not? I mean, you live on a horse farm! How can you say—"

Cindy cut Heather off before she could finish. "I may live there, but none of it's mine." She paused for a minute, studying Heather's face. Would the girl look down on her for being a foster child? Somehow, Cindy didn't think so. Before she knew it, she found herself pouring out the whole story to Heather. She told her all about her previous foster homes, running away, ending up asleep in the orphan foals' stall and being found by Samantha. "So, you see, the McLeans are just my foster parents," she finished.

"That's okay," Heather said. "They sound like the best foster parents you could ask for."

Cindy grinned. She felt better having confided in someone, and Heather obviously had a way of looking on the bright side. Soon they were back on the topic of horses. Riding was an endless subject, and they chatted easily. All too soon, the bell rang for the next period. As the girls headed for their lockers together, Cindy decided to invite Heather to come over and see the place for herself. Then she stopped herself. She still felt like a guest at the McLeans'—a very lucky guest—and she didn't want to do anything that would annoy them even the slightest bit.

That afternoon, Cindy ran all the way down the long, curving driveway to the house. She couldn't wait to see the horses again. She flung down her book bag, whipped off her school clothes, yanked on her jeans and paddock boots, grabbed an apple and headed for the barn. Inside she found Ashleigh giving one of the yearlings a sponge bath.

"How was the first day?" Ashleigh asked.

Cindy offered her apple core to the yearling who munched it happily. "Actually, it wasn't that bad, considering. I did meet a nice girl who's a great artist."

"See, you've already made friends," Ashleigh said. Then, as if reading Cindy's mind, she asked, "Have you come for a ride?"

Cindy nodded eagerly. "If that's okay."

"Of course it's okay. Bo Jangles is free if you want to take him."

"Great," Cindy said, going to get the tack.

Soon she was mounted and heading out once again to the acres of winding trails behind the barn. Automatically, she checked her seat, reminding herself to keep her heels down, to sit lightly but firmly, and to follow the horse's mouth with her hands. She knew she didn't look anywhere as good as Samantha yet, but she felt more confident every day that she rode. Today seemed especially beautiful since she had had to spend half of it indoors. Her cheeks glowed with joy as she cantered to the far end of the property, past white-fenced paddocks and copses of woodland.

Before she knew it, she had reached a wooded hilltop and the boundary between Whitebrook and the neighboring farm. Cindy remembered hearing that the farm had recently changed hands. She wondered idly if the new neighbors had settled in yet. Cindy drew Bo to a halt and looked down to the wood-fenced pasture below them. Suddenly Bo Jangles pricked up his ears intently. In the next moment, a horse whinnied a greeting to them from the pasture. Cindy inhaled sharply as she studied the horse. Its beauty astounded her. He was a gorgeous dapple gray, with a finely shaped head and a flowing darker gray mane and tail. His muscles rippled under his shining coat.

"Let's go over and say hello, boy," Cindy said, urging the gelding forward. She rode up to the fence and peered over.

From what Cindy had been learning about conformation, she suspected the horse was nearly perfect. He had clean lines, a sloping shoulder, and a deep girth. And he was tall—she guessed almost sixteen hands. She gazed at him appreciatively for several minutes before reluctantly asking Bo Jangles to move on.

"We'd better be going, boy, but I promise we'll come back for a visit." With that, Cindy headed the gelding toward the woods. At the trailhead she paused, turning for a final look at the lovely horse. She saw two men approach the horse's paddock. The gray horse began prancing nervously, snorting as he eyed the two men. The older man's lips were turned down in a hardened frown, and he clenched his hands into fists as he walked. The younger man had the same hardened features, but instead of frowning, he wore an arrogant sneer on his face.

As soon as the gray horse heard them approaching, he spun around. At the sight of them, he began to trot nervously in circles. Cindy tightened her grip on the reins to keep Bo Jangles quiet so she could watch the proceedings from her hidden vantage point. When the men came closer, the gray broke into a gallop, his eyes rolling wildly. What Cindy saw next made her heart pound. To catch the horse, the men backed him into a corner, shouting gruffly and waving their arms. As soon as they caught him, they thrust a severe curb bit into his mouth, yanking the bridle over his ears. A saddle was thrown onto his trembling back, and the younger man mounted.

The older man stood in the middle of the paddock, holding a longe line and whip. Every time the rider gave an aid to go forward, the other man whipped the horse's hocks. When he wanted to stop, the rider yanked viciously on the reins until the horse's head was twisted around in pain. In a matter of seconds, the horse was tossing his head up and down to escape the cruel bit, and his coat was covered in lather. Despite the treatment, he seemed to be trying to do what the men wanted. His ears flicked back nervously, hoping for a signal he understood.

"Get up there!" the older man yelled. "Quit your fooling around! We'll teach you to behave!"

A sick, horrified feeling came over Cindy. She had never seen a horse treated like this at Whitebrook. She wanted to yell down to the men to stop, but she was afraid. She couldn't tear herself away from the dreadful scene, either. As she watched the gray going helplessly around and around, her heart went out to him. She felt as if she were on fire with rage and might explode any minute. Close to tears, she watched the man dismount, finally, untack the horse, and let him go. Neither man made any effort to walk the sweat-lathered horse to cool him out. They turned and left the paddock, the younger one carrying the tack; the older man coiling the long whip. The gray ran to the end of the pasture and paced back and forth, stopping every so often to cock an ear in fear.

The minute the men had disappeared, Cindy urged Bo Jangles down the hill to the paddock. She jumped off and coaxed the terrified gray horse forward, fishing in her pocket for the carrots she had learned to keep there. The gray pricked up his ears warily, sidling away. Then the low, gentle voice that Cindy used caught his attention. Timidly, he came forward and allowed her to stroke his neck while he munched the carrot. His coat was dripping wet and hot to touch. Cindy frowned angrily. She wasn't an

20

expert horsewoman, but she did know about animals, and this horse was being abused. She had seen it with her own eyes. She felt helpless with rage that people could treat a beautiful horse so cruelly. The helpless feeling was familiar. "It's not fair!" she whispered to the gray. "Why do you have to live here, with people you don't like, just like I had to live with the Hadleys. If you were mine, I'd take good care of you. I wish you could come to Whitebrook with me. We could have so much fun together . . . " Cindy's voice trailed off wistfully. She did glance around the paddock to see if there was some way she could slip out with the gray, but she knew she was just dreaming. If she had learned one thing from being in her last foster home, it was that stealing didn't help anything. A few months before she had come to Whitebrook, Cindy had been caught shoplifting.

She could remember the day as if it were yesterday. It had been the day after her birthday, and, as usual, her foster parents had forgotten the date. All month long, Cindy had been hinting that she wanted a poster of a puppy and a kitten from a local store. She wanted to hang it above her bed so that she could fall asleep thinking of animals because animals made her happy. She had been told that if she behaved, she might get it for a birthday gift. But the day had come and gone without even so much as a "happy birthday." Then the kids had teased her at school because nobody had brought in cupcakes for the class, like other students' mothers did on their birthdays. Cindy had walked home, crying blindly. She had told herself that she would just go into the store and look at the poster. But when she saw the adorable faces of the animals, she just had to have it. She desperately craved something to comfort her in her loneliness. Without thinking, she had slipped the tube into her school bag. The rest had been a nightmare. The memory of the alarm bell sounding, the store owner screaming, and the police coming to take her home in shame made Cindy break out into a cold sweat. Of course, it hadn't been a real arrest since she was a minor. But it had been a lesson she would never forget.

She knew the people from the Child Protection Services had told the McLeans about the incident. Thankfully, they had never brought it up. They must trust her, she thought. After all, if they thought she was a thief, they wouldn't want her around. The barns were filled with valuable horses and equipment. Anyway, she had shoplifted once and only once. She knew how much one rash act could complicate her life. No matter how upset she was about the treatment of this horse, she wouldn't do anything stupid.

Cindy gazed at the gray sadly. "I can't take you away, boy. Not after all the great things that have happened to me here. I can't risk getting in trouble. But I swear I won't let you down. Those men are mistreating you, and I'm going to find some way to get you help," she vowed. With a sigh, she remounted Bo Jangles. Slowly, she turned and headed for the farm.

On the way back, she thought about what to do. Obviously she had to tell *someone* about what she had seen. But everyone at the farm was so busy with training for the fall races. Should she tell Samantha and her foster parents? Or Mike and Ashleigh? What if they thought she was overreacting? After all, she didn't have their experience and knowledge of horses. Chances were, too, that there wouldn't be anything they could do. Horses were like foster children, Cindy thought unhappily. They ended up where they ended up, and they had no say in the matter.

"Wait a minute," Cindy told herself aloud. "The McLeans fought for me when they knew I was unhappy. They kept me from having to go back to the awful Hadleys. This horse needs my help, just like I needed theirs, and I'm going to help him." No matter what, she decided. Even if it would be safer to mind her own business.

23

Back at the barn, Cindy untacked Bo Jangles, gave him a quick once-over with a curry comb and body brush, and put him in his stall. Len was sweeping the aisle when she finished. "Have you seen my foster dad or Mike or Ashleigh?" Cindy asked the stable manager.

"They're over in the broodmare barn," Len replied.

Cindy hurried over to the mares' barn. She could hear her foster father's voice coming from the direction of the isolation stall at the end of the aisle. "The only solution is to keep the sick mare isolated and hope none of the other horses catch it," he was saying.

The group turned when Cindy appeared. "Hi, Cindy," Samantha said.

Cindy saw the worried expressions on everyone's faces. "What's going on? Is something the matter?" she asked, suddenly afraid.

"The new brood mare that Mike bought in New York arrived with a fever," Samantha explained at Cindy's puzzled expression.

"Will she be okay?" Cindy asked anxiously.

"With treatment, yes," Mr. McLean answered. "The problem is protecting the other stock. We're going to have to sterilize everything that's touched her. We'll keep her in the isolation stall for the time being. No one is to feed or groom her without scrubbing his or her hands afterward. Her blankets, brushes, buckets have to stay completely separate," the trainer said. "If the bacteria got near the training barn . . . "

"It *won't*, Dad," Samantha assured her father. "Consider things taken care of. We'll start sterilizing all the buckets and brushes right now. Cindy, want to give me a hand?"

"Sure," Cindy replied.

Cindy followed Samantha to the store room. She could imagine how frightening a barnful of sick horses would be. Now wasn't the time to tell Samantha or her foster father about the gray horse. It would be thoughtless. They already had enough on their minds. She would have to wait.

When they finally sat down to dinner, everyone seemed tired, and the meal began in relative silence. Cindy glanced awkwardly at her plate. She wished there was something she could do to lighten the mood.

Beth was the first to speak. "I know you're all worried about that mare," she said brightly, "but I'm going to put my foot down for once: no more horse talk tonight. In case you've forgotten, it was Cindy's first day of school today, and I want to hear how it went."

"Oh, Cindy! I'm sorry!" Samantha blurted out. "With the news in the barn, I completely forgot to ask."

Cindy blushed at the apology.

"So how did it go?" her foster father asked kindly.

Cindy began to speak slowly, but with the family's prompting, she soon found herself chatting away about classes and teachers. The talk seemed to cheer them up and take their minds off the sick horse.

"Did you make any new friends?" Mr. McLean asked.

Cindy nodded eagerly. "I did. Her name's Heather and she's a great artist. She draws horses amazingly well. Actually," Cindy continued, after a pause, "I was wondering if maybe I could invite her over one day. She loves riding, too." She practically held her breath while awaiting their answer.

"If she loves riding, then *we'd* love to meet her," Samantha said. "If I don't have class, we could all go on a trail ride together."

"Great idea, and be sure to show her around the farm," Mr. Mclean added.

Cindy felt a warm rush of happiness at the McLeans' eagerness to include her. She finished her dinner contentedly. Then her mind flashed back to her afternoon ride. She *owed* it to the neglected horse to say something. He needed her help. "Since you mentioned trails . . . " she began timidly. She looked around at the McLeans who were beaming at her. They looked so pleased at her request to bring a friend home that she couldn't bring herself to spoil the mood. "I think Heather would love to go on a trail ride," she finished lamely.

"Good. Then it's settled. You're inviting her. Tell her that I'll drive her home afterward," Beth put in.

"Why not make it this week?" Samantha asked, getting up to stack the plates.

"Great!" Cindy answered.

After dinner, Cindy helped clean up. She decided she would talk to Samantha about the horse as soon as the dishes were done. Samantha could help her decide whether it was worth telling her foster parents, too. Before the plates were even dry, though, Tor Nelson, Samantha's blond-haired boyfriend, knocked on the door. Samantha and Tor had been dating for several years and had a lot in common, including their love of horses and riding.

Tor greeted everyone with a smile as he walked into the kitchen.

"Gotta go," Samantha announced. "Great dinner, Beth. Dad, see you at the barn bright and early. And you, too, Cindy."

Cindy watched the attractive pair leave the cottage and walk to Tor's car. She heaved a sigh. She was sure to be asleep by the time Samantha returned. Once again, the gray horse would have to wait.

The next morning, Cindy was up at dawn to help with the chores. Her dreams had been haunted by the gray horse and the abuse he'd received from the men. She worried about him as she went about her jobs— feeding, watering, and mucking out stalls. Refined Thoroughbred heads appeared over the stall doors to whicker a hungry greeting to her. Here and there, she paused to pat a favorite's neck or stroke a nose, working her way down one aisle and up the next.

When she came to the stall that housed the twin orphan foals, Cindy lingered for several minutes. It was wonderful to see the babies growing up into healthy weanlings. She remembered the night she had first come to Whitebrook when she had run away from her old foster parents. She had looked into all of the stalls, hoping to find a place where she could hide. The twin foals' faces had looked so sweet and inviting that she had curled right up beside them and dozed off to sleep. Ever since then, she had kept a close watch on them.

"You think of any names yet?" Len asked.

Cindy spun around, smiling. Since the foals had been born, everyone on the farm had been trying to come up with the perfect names for the two of them. Shaking her head, Cindy said, "Sorry, Len—nothing

I've thought of is anywhere near good enough for these two."

"Well, they can't be no-names forever," Len said, "so keep thinking."

Cindy promised that she would. She spent a few more minutes with the foals, then moved on down the aisle. Her eyes took in every pleasing detail of the stable, down to the shining brass nameplates on the stall doors. If only the beautiful gray horse could have been stabled at Whitebrook, Cindy thought with a stab. He could have a roomy box stall of his own with deep bedding and plenty of sunlight, and she could take care of him. . . . Abruptly, she shook her head to banish the wistful thought. Dreaming wasn't going to help the gray. As soon as she was finished, she went to help tack up the horses who were scheduled for morning workouts.

"You're looking like a real pro," Vic Teleski complimented her as she swung a saddle deftly onto the back of a two-year-old. "My job's getting easier every day."

Cindy grinned at the groom. He, too, had taught her a lot since she had come to Whitebrook, and she loved to be of help to him in any way she could. "I wish I could do this all day instead of just in the mornings, Vic," Cindy said, glancing at her watch. "Oh, look! I'm almost late already." Hurriedly, she

29

gathered up her book bag and ran for the bus, leaving Vic to finish tacking up the colt.

Cindy was actually eager to go so that she could talk to Heather again. She had decided to tell Heather, at least, about the gray horse. She hoped Heather would have an idea about what to do. As she stared out the window of the bus at the rolling fields of Kentucky bluegrass, she vowed again that she wouldn't let the beautiful animal down.

She didn't see Heather again until the period just before lunch, when they both found themselves in a different, lower-level French class. Heather sat down at the desk in front of Cindy. As the teacher called the class to order, she whispered, "Watch—I'll draw your picture." Whenever she could, Cindy stole a glance at Heather's desk. Before too long, Heather held up her notebook. She had drawn an excellent picture of a horse and rider clearing a huge fence with inches to spare.

Cindy grinned when she saw it. "I wish!" she whispered to Heather who grinned back.

After class, the two girls walked to lunch together. "Looks like this is becoming our regular table, huh?" Heather said, as they sat down at the same place they had sat the day before.

Cindy smiled briefly, but was too worked up for small talk, so without wasting any time, she recounted what she had seen on her trail ride. Heather's expression changed from curiosity to shock to anger.

"How could anyone treat a beautiful animal like that? It's a crime!" she said indignantly. "And you're right—you *have* to do something. I'm just not sure what."

"Me, either," Cindy said glumly. Then, brightening, she added, "But maybe if you saw him for yourself you'd have a better idea." Excitedly, she invited Heather to come out to Whitebrook to see the farm and go riding.

"Do you mean it?" Heather asked breathlessly. A spot of color bloomed on her pale cheeks.

"Absolutely. In fact, can you come tomorrow?" Cindy asked.

"Tomorrow?" Heather repeated incredulously.

"That's right—after school. And stay for dinner. My foster mother can drive you home afterward," Cindy added.

"We'll really go riding? On a Thoroughbred farm?" Heather asked.

"All afternoon, if you want," Cindy said.

Heather clapped her hands, speechless with excitement.

3

To Cindy's delight, the next day dawned warm and sunny. A light breeze played at the treetops, ruffling her blond hair as she did her chores. It would be a perfect afternoon for riding. Running to catch the bus, she hugged herself in anticipation. From Len, she had learned that the sick broodmare had improved slightly over the night and, as far as they could tell, no other horses had become infected. There would still be extra work for the staff, who would have to medicate her twice daily and keep a watchful eye on her, but the general mood about her recovery was optimistic.

After school, Heather joined Cindy on Cindy's bus. This time, Cindy didn't notice the chattering around her—she was too busy keeping up her own non-stop conversation with her new friend. When the two girls got off at Whitebrook, Heather looked around in awe.

"I know how you feel," Cindy said, noticing Heather's shining eyes. "I felt the same way when I saw this place for the first time."

"It's—it's incredible," Heather breathed, her eyes taking in the rolling hills, shady oaks, and the lush pastures dotted with horses of all colors—bays, grays, chestnuts, blacks.

"It's even better up close," Cindy promised. "Come on—race you to the house!" With that, Cindy took off down the driveway toward the small cottage near the Reeses' neat white farmhouse she could almost call "home."

"Phew!" Heather exclaimed, following Cindy into the kitchen. "Good thing it was a tie or we'd have to have a rematch."

Although Beth was in Lexington teaching her aerobics class, she had left a note on the table. *"Cindy: There's a pitcher of lemonade in the fridge and a plate of oatmeal cookies in the pantry for you and Heather. See you later—and have fun!—Beth"* Reading the note, Cindy felt a lump forming in her throat. She couldn't remember anyone ever caring for her so much. She turned away for a second so that Heather wouldn't see how affected she was by the simple, motherly gesture.

After wolfing down the snack, the girls went to change into their riding clothes in Cindy's room. Cindy couldn't help but notice how frayed Heather's jodhpurs were. They looked like the clothes she had worn before the McLeans had insisted on buying her a new wardrobe—threadbare and a little too small. She knew that old jodhpurs didn't affect how you rode one bit—after all, the horses couldn't tell the difference—but she felt her heart going out to Heather all the same.

"You guys going to take all day up there?" a cheery voice called.

"No way, Sammy! We've already wasted enough time in school!" Cindy called back. She and Heather hurried downstairs to the kitchen where Samantha was waiting.

"Heather, meet Samantha McLean, groom, exercise rider, and owner of the amazing Shining," Cindy said with a flourish. She was thrilled that Samantha was free that afternoon and able to join them.

Samantha greeted Heather warmly. At first, Heather just nodded shyly. Cindy had warned the McLeans that she tended to be kind of quiet. As they headed out to tour the barns, Samantha told Heather about some of the famous residents of the farm— Fleet Goddess, Wonder, Wonder's Pride.

All at once, Heather spoke up excitedly. "Gosh, I didn't know this was the same Whitebrook Farm that owned Pride. I read about him in *The Racing Form* when he was named Horse of the Year. He sounded really impressive."

"We'll introduce you to all of them," Samantha promised. "And I'll show you my filly, Shining."

"I can't wait," Heather replied. "Cindy said Shining won a big race at Saratoga this summer."

Cindy stared wordlessly as her friend talked amiably with Samantha, utterly surprised by the reserved girl's sudden transformation into a chatty, relaxed horseperson. She seemed so different from the shy, awkward girl Cindy had met at school. Cindy smiled, remembering that she, too, turned into a different person under Whitebrook's spell.

"Hello, girls, we've brought visitors," Samantha announced to the horses, as they entered the broodmare barn. She and Cindy led Heather slowly down the aisle, introducing her to the mares as they went.

"Here's Wonder," Samantha said, gesturing to a gleaming, copper-colored mare. Wonder wakened from her afternoon doze and stuck her head over her stall door to see what was going on.

"She was Ashleigh Griffen's first race horse," Cindy explained to Heather. "Wonder almost died at birth, but Ashleigh saved her, and she went on to win the Kentucky Derby and set all kinds of track records."

"And now her offspring are carrying on her name," Samantha added, describing Townsend Princess and Mr. Wonderful who would soon begin yearling training. "Right now Wonder is in foal again."

Heather stroked the mare's neck gently, listening with rapt attention to Samantha and Cindy's recounting of Wonder's glorious achievements. "So I guess she's what you could call a Supermom, huh?" Heather asked when they had finished.

"Definitely," Cindy replied, chuckling with Samantha, "and so is Fleet Goddess." She walked a couple of stalls down to show Heather the nearly black mare. "She's another one of Ashleigh's big winners."

Goddess poked her nose inquisitively toward the group. Heather reached up to rub the white star in the middle of her forehead. "What a pretty face you have," she remarked.

"Isn't it?" Samantha agreed. "Her first baby, Precocious, who's also a yearling now, inherited that same white triangle. It's really eye-catching. And who knows? Maybe it's a good luck marking, too. Fleeting Moment, her second foal, has a tiny white star, too."

"Is Goddess in foal again, too?" Heather asked.

Samantha nodded. "Mike bred her to his stallion Jazzman again because he's so happy with the way Precocious has turned out. She and Wonder will foal in late winter or early spring," Samantha said. She explained that while all registered Thoroughbreds have their official birthday on January 1st, their real birthdays could, of course, come as late as May. In order to have good-sized yearlings, breeders hoped for January and February foals. "Sometimes the plan doesn't always work, though," Samantha continued. "Mares can't always be bred when the breeder would like. The good stallions have to be booked, and mares don't always conceive at the first breeding session."

Heather nodded, her eyes bright with interest. "So what happens to the foals born in late spring?"

"The younger foals usually have caught up in size by the time they're two-year-olds—but not always. Those that don't are given more time to mature before starting serious training."

"Sounds like you've covered just about every-thing, huh?"

The three girls looked up to see Len, followed by Mr. Reese, entering the barn. Samantha shot the two men a grin. "Not quite *everything*," she said, "but it is nice to have an appreciative audience." She turned to introduce Heather.

Cindy was pleased to see that Heather, smiling, politely shook hands with the stable manager and the co-owner of Whitebrook. With her own troubled past, Cindy tended to be defensive rather than cordial when she met new people. It wasn't that she meant to be rude, she just simply didn't trust anyone until she really got to know them.

After finishing the tour of the broodmare barn, the little group went to watch the weanlings and yearlings playing outside in the pastures. As usual, the antics of the young, impish fillies and colts delighted their observers. Cindy pointed out Fleeting Moment, Goddess's newer foal, in the weanling field, as well as the twin orphan foals. "They're adorable!" Heather exclaimed.

"'Adorable' ... hmmm ... " Cindy repeated. "No, it's good but not quite right." At Heather's puzzled expression, Cindy laughed. "We're still trying to think up names for them, so whenever anyone says anything, I try it out."

"If I think of any good names, I'll let you know," Heather promised.

Continuing the tour, Cindy showed Heather Precocious and Mr. Wonderful, who were turned out with the other yearlings.

"Wow! They really look like their dams," Heather commented.

Samantha nodded. "Uh-huh, and now you can see Precocious's sire, too," she said, leading them toward the smallest of the three barns.

Heather found at least as much to exclaim over in the stallion barn where Whitebrook sensations Wonder's Pride and Jazzman were standing at stud, but she was overcome with excitement by the training barn. She gasped aloud at the busy stable. "Wow! Real race horses!" she breathed, her eyes fixed on a pair of two-year-olds that Len was leading out into the yard.

"There are more horses inside." Once again, Cindy introduced the awestruck Heather to the horses one-by-one, saving Shining for last.

"It's a true honor to meet you," Heather said solemnly to the roan filly.

Shining pricked up her ears, happy for the attention, and whuffled a greeting. "She says, 'The pleasure is all mine,'" Samantha translated, grinning. "Listen, since we're here, why don't we get Shining and two of the exercise horses tacked up and go for a ride?"

Heather grinned from ear to ear at the suggestion. After tacking up Bo Jangles and a trusty Appaloosa named Chips for Heather, they joined Samantha in the stable yard. A few fair-weather clouds had blown in, dotting the brilliant Kentucky sky with patches of white. Once they had mounted and set off for the trail, Cindy took in the now-familiar scene of sparkling white fences, brick-red barns, and vast acres of rolling pastureland. The view from horseback was her favorite, and she felt almost overcome by the beauty of the day. Stealing a glance at Heather, she could tell that her friend felt the same way.

The girls trotted along for several minutes, slowing to a walk when the terrain roughened. Cindy took advantage of the slower pace to tell Samantha about the gray horse on the neighboring farm. She had been waiting for the right time, and this seemed like the perfect opportunity. Samantha listened attentively. "I just know he's being abused," Cindy concluded, after relating how frightened of the men he had seemed.

Samantha frowned. "The people who live there just moved in. No one knows much about them. They keep to themselves. But we might as well ride over there and take a look."

When they reached the wooded hill above the neighboring farm, Samantha suggested they ride down closer to the fenced paddock and the farm house and barn beyond. "I'm going to ride down to the house and see if anyone's around," she said. "Since we're neighbors, I should introduce myself." Cindy had her doubts about how friendly the two men would be, but she felt relieved that Samantha was taking charge of the situation.

While Samantha headed off toward the farm buildings, Cindy and Heather edged closer to the field. There was nobody in sight. The big, beautiful gray was grazing quietly in the paddock. He lifted his head and pricked up his ears at their approach. He paused, uneasily sniffing the air, then snorted warily.

"It's okay, boy. It's only us," Cindy murmured, coaxing him closer.

In a minute or two, the horse seemed reassured. He walked over to the fence, nickering to the other horses. As he came closer, Samantha rode into sight. "The place is shut up tighter than a drum," she said. "You can't ride any closer than the edge of this field because it's surrounded by fences." She halted Shining next to the paddock. The filly pushed her nose out assertively to touch noses with the now inquisitive gray. She squealed happily at making a new acquaintance. Cindy watched the scene quietly. Once again, she felt awed by the horse's beauty. She had been studying a conformation book she had found in the stable office, and she was more impressed than ever with the gray's lines.

As if reading Cindy's thoughts, Samantha commented admiringly, "He's a beauty all right— good conformation. I can see why you like him."

41

"I think he's gorgeous," Heather said softly. "He has such a noble head and those big, big eyes."

Samantha cast an appraising eye over the horse, then lifted his lips to check his teeth. "He can't be much older than two," she speculated. "I wonder what the new owners are going to do with him—race him? Breed him? With looks like that, he must have good bloodlines."

"When I was here before, it looked like they were trying to train him," Cindy said. "They had him tacked up and going around on a longe line. But they were using force—too much force. They were jerking the reins and cracking the whip at him. When they caught him, they cornered him instead of shaking some grain to get him to come. They didn't even brush him. They just threw the saddle and bridle on and didn't cool him out afterward even though he was lathered with sweat."

Samantha pursed her lips thoughtfully. "It's funny," she began, "he looks healthy and fit—as if he'd been well cared for." She paused. "Are you sure they were treating him that badly, Cindy? Sometimes it's hard to tell what's going on from a distance, and you were all the way back at the trail entrance."

Cindy looked at the horse. She knew what Samantha was saying made sense. He *did* look like the picture of health and good care, not like an abused animal. If only the two men had been there, she could have shown Samantha what she meant. She stared at the ground for a minute or two. "I wasn't imagining it," she said finally. "He was afraid of them."

Samantha nodded. "It probably wouldn't be a bad idea if you rode over here once in a while to check up on him. Though you know there isn't really anything we can do. He's not our horse, Cin. And unless they saw real abuse, my father and Mike and Ashleigh wouldn't dare interfere with other trainers just because they didn't like their training methods. That's a good way to make permanent enemies in the business, not to mention the fact that it makes you look foolish when they turn around and beat your horses with their 'inferior' methods."

"But—" Cindy tried to interrupt.

"When you have a horse like this one," Samantha continued, "I can't believe any owner or trainer would deliberately abuse him. It would be like cutting your nose to spite your face."

Samantha was an experienced horsewoman whose opinion Cindy respected too much to challenge. Still, she felt a nagging doubt about the men's training methods. She knew what she had seen: the beautiful gray had been terrified.

After a leisurely ride back to the stables, the three

43

girls untacked the horses and cooled them out. Samantha had to leave shortly afterward to meet some friends in town. Left alone, Cindy and Heather decided to clean some tack to surprise Samantha and Len. As she soaped a pair of reins, Cindy brooded silently over her dilemma. She stared at her sponge, thinking hard.

"You know, I don't mean to doubt Samantha," Heather said, "but we saw how nervous he was when we came up to the paddock. Samantha didn't because she was checking on the farm. He didn't act like a horse who had a lot of trust in people."

Cindy looked up. "That's what I thought," she said with a frown. She felt relieved that Heather didn't think she'd been imagining things.

"If Samantha had seen how shy he was at first, she might not have thought you were overreacting," Heather added.

"The sad thing is that even if we are right, Sammy's right, too: there's nothing we can do unless we can prove they're abusing him," Cindy pointed out. "He's not ours. I think that's why she didn't want us to get more involved."

Heather was silent while she oiled the saddle she was working on. "We'll just have to wait and see, I guess. If you see something like you saw before, tell me, okay?"

Cindy nodded. After the afternoon's activities, she felt a closer bond to her new friend. They shared a profound love for horses, and, what was more, they thought alike, too. Best of all, Cindy thought, it was wonderful to be able to share Whitebrook with a friend her own age. Together, the two of them might come up with some way of helping the gray colt. . . .

4

AUTUMN AT WHITEBROOK WAS ALWAYS A FULL SEASON, and this one was no exception. With school, helping out in the barn, practicing her own riding, doing homework, and pitching in around the house, Cindy found herself busier than ever before. She fell into bed, exhausted, at the end of the day, and on more than one occasion, Samantha or Beth had to wake her up and tell her to change out of the clothes she had fallen asleep in. Although she was too preoccupied to give her own situation much thought, at the back of her mind, Cindy knew that she was happier than she had ever been. With each passing day, she felt more at home at Whitebrook, more a part of the family, and more a part of the well-oiled racing machine that the farm was.

She had made it a point to learn everything she could about the fall racing schedule. Samantha was eager to fill her in. After her sensational performance at Saratoga, Shining was being readied for the Grade 1 Beldame Stakes at Belmont in early October. "It's a big race for fillies and mares who are three-years-old and up," Samantha explained one afternoon, as she and Cindy sat on a hay bale outside of Shining's stall, poring over the *Racing Form*. "And at one and one-eighth miles it will be a fair test."

"Will other good fillies be racing?" Cindy asked.

Samantha nodded. "The race is drawing some of the best fillies and mares in the country. And that includes Her Majesty."

Cindy didn't miss the ominous tone in Samantha's voice when she mentioned Lavinia Townsend's horse. From the stories she had heard, Cindy knew that with the Townsends involved, anything could happen. "I know Shining will beat her. Am I right, girl?" she asked, getting up to rub the pretty roan face. "You'll show those Townsends. You did it before, and you'll do it again." Since their return from Saratoga, Cindy had continued to help Samantha with the filly's grooming. Samantha was thrilled with the extra help. Her mornings were already hectic since she rode so many horses during their daily workouts.

"I hope so, too," Samantha said. "Now, let's give you that lesson, Cindy, before we're both too busy to sneak out for half an hour."

Under Samantha's tutelage—as well as Ashleigh's, Mike's, Len's and just about anyone who stopped by the ring when she happened to be riding—Cindy had made great strides in her riding in a short time. Today Samantha was full of praise and encouragement. After a thirty-minute session of flat work, she called to Cindy. "I think it's almost time you learned to jump," Samantha said. "We'll have to get Tor to come over and give you a few pointers soon." Samantha's boyfriend was a top jump rider and had competed several times at the National Horse Show.

"That would be great," Cindy said, her face glowing, as she jumped neatly to the ground.

Walking Bo Jangles back to his stall in the training barn, the girls noticed a small group gathered at the end of the aisle. "Oh, no, not them," Samantha murmured through clenched teeth when she caught sight of Brad and Lavinia Townsend. "Unfortunately we have to keep dealing with them if we want to find out how Townsend Princess is doing. I'm going to see what they're up to. As soon as Ashleigh starts Mr. Wonderful's training, they'll be over here all the time. Why don't you put Bo away and ignore them?"

Cindy followed Samantha's advice. She led Bo

quietly into his stall, untacking and grooming him there instead of on the cross-ties. Then she slipped quietly into Shining's stall to give her a quick brushing. From inside, she could just make out Samantha, Lavinia and Brad, and Brad's father, Clay.

"Ash told me he'll start his yearling training this week," Mr. Townsend said.

"That's what she plans," Samantha responded.

Lavinia gave an arrogant toss of her perfectly coiffed blond hair, causing Mr. Wonderful to back into his stall in surprise. "I still think he should be trained at Townsend Acres. We have much better facilities."

Samantha ignored her but placed herself between Lavinia and the yearling.

"Ashleigh and I have already reached a decision," Mr. Townsend responded to his daughter-in-law. "By the way," he added to Samantha, "how's your filly doing?"

"She's fit and healthy and well-rested, and we're putting her back in training for the Beldame." Cindy smiled, knowing that Lavinia had never gotten over Shining's beating her filly, Her Majesty, at Saratoga.

The Townsends and Samantha started walking down the aisle. Cindy looked up from her grooming to see Lavinia staring in over Shining's stall door.

"What's this?" Lavinia asked haughtily. "Are you

49

breaking child labor laws at Whitebrook now? That groom is much too young to work here," she said, pointing a long, red nail at Cindy.

"You met Cindy before, didn't you?" Samantha asked.

"Did I? I don't really remember."

"Well, this is Cindy Blake. I guess you could say she's a new member of the family. Beth and Dad have just become her foster parents," Samantha explained.

"Foster parents?" Lavinia looked at Samantha in amazement. "Are you kidding? You're taking in orphans? Well, I have to hand it to you—you sure are brave." She glanced at Cindy again with distaste, then continued, "You never know what an orphan will do. *I* certainly wouldn't want to take the risk." With a shudder, Lavinia turned on her heel and clicked haughtily down the aisle, motioning for Brad to follow her.

While Lavinia was making her speech, Cindy's cheeks had grown red with anger and humiliation. As soon as she was gone, Cindy ran blindly out of the barn toward the house, choking back sobs as she went. Lavinia couldn't have hurt her more if she had planned it. The woman's harsh words made her reel with anger.

Samantha caught up with her at the door. She put an arm around Cindy's shaking shoulders. "Don't you dare listen to a single word that—that nasty, stupid woman said! If there's one thing she knows less about than horses, it's people. She's a complete spoiled brat and a snob. You can't pay any attention to her. Okay? Promise?"

Cindy looked up, biting her lip to stop from crying. "I'll try not to," she promised.

"If it makes you feel any better, when Shining first got here, Lavinia said that she ought to be sent to the glue factory," Samantha said.

In spite of herself, Cindy smiled. "Obviously, she doesn't know quality when she sees it," she said, putting on her best imitation of Lavinia's snobby accent.

"You've got that right," Samantha agreed, shaking her head ruefully.

It would have been better for the girls to avoid seeing the Townsends altogether, as every meeting involving Brad or Lavinia was bound to be frustrating or upsetting. But since Ashleigh and Samantha were determined to see Townsend Princess—and Cindy was determined to go with them—the three of them often drove over to Townsend Acres when they had a spare moment. Ken Maddock was in charge of the filly's training, and he was prepping her for a couple of possible fall races, including two October races, the Frizette Stakes for two-year-old fillies at Belmont and the Breeders' Futurity for two-year-olds at Keeneland.

"Looks fit as a fiddle, doesn't she?" the head trainer remarked as Ashleigh, Sam, and Cindy stood beside the track rail watching one of the exercise riders breeze Princess a quarter mile.

Ashleigh nodded. "Sure does. I'm still amazed at how quickly she healed from her injury, and obviously Saratoga didn't take a lot out of her. Still, as well as she's training, I don't think she has the seasoning or experience yet for us to even consider entering her in the Breeders' Cup Juvenile."

"I agree," Maddock replied. "Next year is time enough to think of the classic races."

Cindy listened attentively, as trainer and jockey discussed Princess's training in detail, going over her workout times, feeding, and anticipated racing schedule. She had vowed to herself to learn as much as she could about training and racing, so that she would be as knowledgeable as possible when she performed her duties at Whitebrook.

Midway through their conversation, Lavinia came sauntering up, her custom-made riding boots glimmering in the sunlight.

"Ken! Ken! I need to talk to you right away about

Her Majesty. It's very important," she finished, eyeing the Whitebrook group coldly.

Ashleigh smiled sympathetically at the trainer. "We'll talk another day, Ken. The girls and I should be on our way, anyway. We'll just say hello to Hank before we go." Hank was an old Townsend Acres groom who had known Ashleigh since she was Cindy's age.

In the racing barn, Hank greeted them cheerfully. "Well, it's about time you stopped by," he said. "Haven't seen head or tail of any of you since Saratoga." Hank stepped away from the horse he was checking over.

Ashleigh explained that they had been busy as usual over at Whitebrook, with Shining's and the yearlings' training and Pride's stud season to take care of.

"It's probably just as well that you can't make it here all the time. Some people," Hank remarked, clearing his throat significantly, "aren't always in the most welcoming moods over here."

"We noticed," Samantha said.

"Lavinia is never overjoyed to see us," Ashleigh added tersely.

Hank lowered his voice. "She's been even worse than usual ever since Her Majesty lost to Shining at Saratoga. She snaps at me and the other grooms as if it was our fault the filly didn't win. About the only thing that stops her complaining is Mr. Townsend's being here. He's the one person she won't talk back to."

"Thank goodness for that," Ashleigh said. "Because she's going to have to get used to our being around here. I intend to keep an eye on Princess whether she likes it or not."

"Be my guest," Hank said. "Just be prepared for some ugly scenes if Mr. Townsend has to go away again."

"I've had plenty of experience with that already," Ashleigh said grimly. Cindy knew from what Samantha and Ashleigh had told her that Clay Townsend often traveled to England to oversee a Thoroughbred breeding operation he was involved in there. Sometimes he could be gone weeks or months. In the past, Lavinia and Brad had used his absences as opportunities to launch underhanded attacks on Whitebrook. So the longer Clay Townsend stayed put, the better. He himself was a tough businessman, but he had never sunk to the shameless scheming of his son and daughter-in-law.

Before the girls headed back to Whitebrook, Hank invited them to watch Her Majesty being breezed with another horse. Cindy noticed that both Ashleigh and Samantha looked more grim than enthusiastic about the prospect. Still, none of them was going to say no to a chance to watch the competition. They headed back out to the training track, resuming their places on the rail. In a few minutes, the gleaming filly could be seen taking her warm-up lap around the oval alongside another horse. When the exercise rider gave her the "go" signal, she sprang forward, flattening out immediately into a racing pace. She whipped by the onlookers at the rail in a blur of mane and pounding hooves.

"What do you think?" Hank asked quietly.

Ashleigh turned to the groom. "I think we've just seen our competition for the Beldame," she said.

THE FOLLOWING SATURDAY, CINDY WAS UP EVEN EARLIER than usual. The yearlings were going to be longed for the first time that morning after the regular morning workouts for the older horses on the oval. Cindy had invited Heather over to watch the workouts and training session with her. As soon as she was up and dressed in her usual weekend garb of jeans and a T-shirt, there was a loud knock on the front door. "Coming, Heather!" Cindy yelled, knowing that nobody else would be showing up at six a.m. on a Saturday.

She ran a comb through her blond hair and trotted downstairs.

"Don't worry. I've let her in," Beth called. Beth had gotten accustomed to the early-to-bed, early-to-rise schedule of the farm.

When Cindy came into the kitchen, she saw that Beth already had Heather seated at the table and was serving her breakfast. Samantha and her father were already up, too. "I could tell just from looking at Heather that she had skipped breakfast," Beth said. "You sit down, too, Cindy, and have something to eat."

Cindy grinned at Heather, who was shoveling eggs and bacon into her mouth at a rapid pace. "Hey, Cindy. I thought I wouldn't be hungry this early, but I was wrong," she said between mouthfuls. Sniffing the air appreciatively, Cindy sat down beside her friend.

As soon as the meal was finished, they all headed outside. Beth had decided to come along and watch, too.

Vic and Len already had two of Mike's horses tacked up and were leading them from the training stable toward the mile oval to the side of the barns. Ashleigh and Mike were with them.

While Beth walked over to join Ashleigh and Mike, Samantha and her father headed into the stable; Samantha to get Shining, and her father to check over and prepare horses he would be working that morning.

Samantha called to Cindy, "I don't need any help. Take Heather over to watch the first workouts."

Cindy led the way to the training oval. Ashleigh was already in the saddle of one of Mike's horses, a two-year-old colt, and was listening intently to her husband as he gave her instructions for the work. After fastening her chin strap, Ashleigh gathered up the reins and urged the colt onto the track and began warming him up. Mike stood at the rail, stop watch in hand. Vic held the second horse, and Len returned to the stables to help Ian McLean.

Cindy glanced over to Heather as they approached the oval. Her face was alight, and she was grinning from ear to ear.

"This is like a dream," she said to Cindy. "I've always loved watching races on TV and reading race results in the paper, but I never thought I'd actually *see* a morning workout! Wow! And these horses are all going to be racing at the big tracks!"

"Not all of them," Cindy replied. "Some of them just don't have the talent."

"What happens to them?" Heather asked with concern.

"Mike and Ashleigh and Mr. Reese keep the fillies and mares for breeding stock. Some of the colts with good bloodlines stay here, and some are sold to other breeders. Tor and Samantha have helped Mike find buyers for a few geldings, who'll be retrained as pleasure horses or jumpers. None of these horses ever go to a bad home."

"That's good to know," Heather said with relief. "Oh, look. Ashleigh's starting to gallop him!"

Cindy saw that Ashleigh had let the bay colt out, and she and the colt were moving up the track at a slow gallop. They sailed around the first turn at an easy, collected pace, with Ashleigh riding slightly out of the saddle in a jockey's crouch. They continuted down the backstretch at the same pace, but when they reached the quarter pole on the far turn, Ashleigh crouched lower over the colt's withers and gave him rein, kneading her hands up along his neck. The colt immediately dug in, lengthening his stride, and he and Ashleigh roared off the turn and down the stretch, breezing out the last quarter mile.

As they swept past the mile marker pole, Ashleigh stood in her stirrups, signaling the colt to drop back into a canter, then a trot. She circled him and headed back to Mike.

"That looked good to me," Heather said excitedly. "I've sure never ridden that fast."

Cindy glanced over to Mike, who was smiling as Ashleigh rode the colt off the oval. "Mike looks happy," she said to Heather. She hadn't watched enough workouts herself to be a real judge of how a horse had performed.

The two girls remained at the rail to watch the other workouts. Samantha took out another horse, but only slow galloped him through two laps. Then Ashleigh rode out one of the seasoned horses that Ian

McLean was training. Mike got into the saddle of another, and they worked the two horses together. Then Samantha rode Shining out.

"This is what I've been waiting for," Heather said, her eyes glowing.

Cindy grinned. "Me, too. I love to watch Shining and Sammy."

Shining didn't disappoint them. She moved with grace and power as Samantha guided her around the oval. To Cindy, the filly was pure poetry in motion. She did everything so effortlessly, and when Samantha set her down to breeze out the last quarter, Shining flew. Her hoofs barely seemed to touch the ground, although Cindy could hear their rhythmic pounding as the filly and Samantha swept by.

"I must be dreaming," Heather said with an enraptured sigh.

Cindy looked over to Ashleigh as Samantha pulled Shining up. Ashleigh was beaming and gave Samantha a thumbs up. "Twenty-two and change!" she called out to Samantha.

"And I wasn't even pushing her," Samantha called back as she rode Shining off the oval. "What a girl you are!" she praised as she patted Shining's neck. Shining bobbed her head as if to say, "I know, but thanks."

Cindy and Heather hurried over as Samantha dismounted and pulled up the stirrup irons. Shining was the last horse to be worked that morning. Len and Vic had already led the other horses off to be cooled out before they were returned to their stalls.

"So what did you think?" Samantha asked Heather.

"It was wonderful! Thank you so much for letting me watch!"

"You're welcome to watch any time you want," Samantha told her.

Vic walked over as Samantha drew the reins over Shining's head and gave the filly a loving kiss on the nose. "I'll cool her out for you," he offered. "I know you want to watch the yearling training."

"Thanks, Vic," Samantha said with a smile, giving Shining a last pat. "Ready, girls?"

"We sure are," Cindy said.

They set out in a group for the walled yearling training ring behind the stable buildings. The six foot wooden walls around the ring were meant to prevent the young horses from being distracted by outside noise and activity.

"Will it be frightening for the yearlings to be longed for the first time?" Cindy asked her foster father as they walked along. She knew that over the past couple of weeks, he and Len, with Samantha and Ashleigh's help, had gently broken the young horses to saddle in a big box stall. They had led the yearlings around so they could get used to the feel of the tack, but none of them had ever seen a longe line. It was a crucial step in their training, teaching them to listen to voice commands and smooth out their gaits.

"It may take them awhile to understand what's expected of them," Ian McLean explained. "But with patience and understanding from us, they'll all catch on. They've never been given any reason to fear or mistrust anyone who's handled them—that's really the first step in training."

"Or as Charlie used to say," Ashleigh added, speaking of Charlie Burke, the much-loved and respected old trainer who had taught her all she knew, "you get more with honey than vinegar."

Ian McLean smiled. "Charlie had it right there, and he should know after all the champions he trained."

Cindy suddenly thought of the gray horse and the treatment she'd seen him receive. Those men certainly weren't using honey. She stole a glance at Heather and could see she was thinking of him, too. "Let's ride out there this afternoon," Cindy whispered as they reached the yearling ring.

Heather nodded. "I think we should, too," she whispered back.

Cindy and Heather watched with rapt interest from the side of the ring with Beth, Samantha, Ashleigh, and Mike as Mr. McLean and Len led the first of the six yearlings into the ring. It was Mr. Wonderful, and Cindy sighed at the beauty of the young colt who was prancing eagerly at the end of the lead shank Len held. His head was high and his ears were pricked as he looked curiously around the ring.

Wonder's son gleamed with health and good care. His copper colored coat glinted like a new penny. Before he could start to fuss, Len clipped the longe line to his halter, then handed it to Mr. McLean. Slowly Mr. McLean stepped back several paces, talking quietly to the colt. Mr. Wonderful eyed the line suspiciously, but with Len at his head to steady him, he stayed calm. From the center Mr. McLean clucked several times, asking the colt to "wa-alk, wa-alk." He held a whip in his hand, but he kept it low on the ground, picking it up ever so slightly to give a command. Len led the horse around in a circle several times to get him used to the idea of longing. When he thought Mr. Wonderful understood, he dropped slowly away. At first, the colt stopped or tried to head to the middle when left on his own. Then Len would appear at his head again and get him moving forward while Mr. McLean repeated the walk command. After several repetitions and restarts, Mr. Wonderful walked obediently at the end of the line, occasionally breaking to prance a few steps.

"He's full of energy, isn't he?" Heather asked.

Cindy nodded, her eyes shining. The yearling was obviously a quick learner, and, now that he had figured out what he was expected to do, he was bored and wanted to run. All the galloping and playing in the yearling pasture had made him fit and frisky. Even at this young age, he was in love with speed.

Before he could get frustrated, Mr. McLean ended the day's session and asked for Precocious to be brought out.

Len came forward leading Precocious. With her coal black coat and shining white triangle on her forehead, the filly was truly striking. When she saw Mr. Wonderful, Precocious whinnied loudly and danced at the end of her lead line.

In reply, Mr. Wonderful snorted loudly. "I'll bet he's telling her to quit showing off and get down to business," Heather ventured.

Cindy laughed. The way Precocious was arching her neck and rolling her eyes, it did look like the filly was trying to attract attention to herself.

Precocious put on much more of a show than Mr. Wonderful had. She played and fussed, balked at the longe line, and whinnied whenever she glimpsed another horse. At one point, she planted her toes in and stared at Mr. McLean, snorting indignantly. With infinite patience, the trainer and Len continued with the lesson until finally Precocious consented to take a few turns around the ring, more or less walking.

Samantha joked to Ashleigh and Mike about who would be the first to ride the temperamental filly. "She'll have most of us off before she's two, if she keeps up like this," Mike said with a chuckle.

"Speak for yourself," Samantha retorted good-naturedly. "I'm sure she just needs a woman's touch. We girls like to stick together, you know."

Cindy smiled. She loved listening to the banter around the stables, and she couldn't help but cherish the hope that someday she would be able to join in— to be an exercise rider herself. So far she had kept her dream to herself; it seemed so impossibly far off that she didn't dare tell anyone.

After the training session, everyone hurried off in different directions, with more chores to be done.

"This place is busier than a beehive," Heather remarked, as she and Cindy tacked up Bo Jangles and Chips for their ride.

"It sure is," Cindy agreed. "And it's about to get even busier. My foster father's leaving on a business trip to Florida this week, Shining's got a race coming up at Belmont soon—I can barely keep it all straight myself. I've been meaning to go check on the gray for days, but I've been so busy helping out that I haven't been able to get away."

"I know how you feel. With all my little brothers and sisters, I don't have much time for anything either," Heather said. After a pause, she added shyly, "I think being at Whitebrook is the most fun I've ever had."

Cindy looked up from tightening Bo Jangles's girth. "Me, too," she said, her throat suddenly dry. She didn't think she'd ever get over her good fortune at ending up at Whitebrook with such wonderful people.

Riding along the now-familiar trail, the two girls chatted happily until they drew near the neighboring property. When they reached the top of the rise, they grew silent. "I almost don't want to look," Cindy said.

"I know," Heather agreed. "I'm too afraid of what we'll see."

The girls' worst fears were confirmed. Peering through the trees at the end of the trail, they saw the same man Cindy had seen her first time out—the older one—in the paddock with the gray horse. Once again, he had the horse on a longe line. The way he was mistreating him was even more obvious since the girls had just come from watching Mr. McLean longe the yearlings. Instead of flicking the whip harmlessly along the ground behind the horse to encourage him, this man was smacking it on the horse's flank over and over, his eyes bloodshot with rage. Squealing in fear, the horse repeatedly broke stride into a canter only to be yanked brutally back to a trot. After enduring several minutes of the abuse, the horse swung his hindquarters around and started backing away from the man. Nothing the man did would induce him to go forward. He reared and twisted to get away from the whip and the harsh bit. Finally the man gave up in disgust. Cursing loudly he threw the whip at the horse in a rage. Then he backed the horse against the fence, unclipped the longe line and yanked the bridle over his head.

Cindy and Heather exchanged desperate glances as the man left the paddock.

"If only we could comfort him somehow!" Heather cried.

"I'd give anything just to be able to pat him and be with him for awhile," Cindy said.

"We can't though. If that man came back and found us—"

Heather didn't have to finish. Cindy could hear Samantha's words echoing in her mind: "My father wouldn't dare interfere with other trainers. That's a good way to make permanent enemies in the business. . . . " Even thinking of upsetting the McLeans or Mike and Ashleigh gave Cindy a sick feeling in her stomach, but surely her foster father wouldn't approve of what was going on here.

Cindy gazed at the gray—he was magnificent, despite his sad treatment. "We need to give this horse a name. What do you think of Glory? He's still glorious, even after all he's been through."

"Oh, yes, he's glorious all right," Heather said.

Riding back, Cindy and Heather discussed their plan of action. Cindy decided to tell her foster parents about what they'd seen. "I think they should at least know what's going on," she said. "And I'd rather tell them myself than bother Samantha about it again. Besides, if we get her to ride out there with us again, Glory is bound to be grazing quietly in the field." Heather agreed that she ought to at least mention it.

That evening, Cindy found her foster father updating training charts in the stable office. He kept meticulous records of all the horses' conditions, times, etc. She knocked timidly to get his attention.

Mr. McLean looked up. His face looked weary, but he managed to smile. "Cindy, what can I do for you?" he asked kindly.

"I'm sorry if I'm interrupting—" she began awkwardly.

"Of course you're not interrupting. I'm just getting organized before I leave for Florida. What's up?"

Before she could lose her nerve, Cindy blurted out what she and Heather had seen that morning at the neighboring farm, adding that it was the second time she'd been witness to the cruel treatment.

Mr. McLean frowned. "Hmm . . . You're right. That doesn't sound good . . . I'll tell you what, I'll try to find out what I can about our neighbors, okay? In fact, I've been meaning to drive over there for a few weeks. I just haven't found the time."

Cindy nodded. She wanted to say more, but the tired lines on her foster father's face stopped her. He was obviously exhausted from the long day and from getting ready for his trip. She bit her lip and headed for the house, praying that he would remember to ask around.

All day Sunday, Cindy wondered if her foster father had found out anything that would shed light on Glory's owners. Finally, after dinner, when she was drying dishes, Mr. McLean mentioned that he had asked several of the locals as well as some business associates what they knew about the farm bordering Whitebrook. "I wasn't able to find out much. No one seems to know anything about them. They keep pretty much to themselves—don't go to town much, and their farm gate stays locked."

Cindy's heart sank at the news. It sounded just like a description of people who might be up to no good.

"Honey," Mr. McLean said gently, "I know you've

been learning fast, but are you sure the horse was being mistreated? Remember that you're still new to the horse world. I think Samantha explained that sometimes training a horse can *look* like abuse when it's really just discipline. Knowing how to use a crop or a whip properly is part of horsemanship, cruel as that may seem."

"I wasn't imagining it," Cindy said quickly and a little defensively. "Heather and I both saw how scared the horse was."

"Well," Mr. McLean said with a sigh, "the fact is, unless I see our neighbor abusing the animal, there's not much I can do."

"Could you come out with us someday?" Cindy said persistently.

"Of course I could," Mr. McLean said generously. "And I will as soon as I get back from Florida, all right?"

Before Cindy could reply, the phone rang. "Ian?" Beth called from upstairs. "It's the Florida people! They want to talk about your meeting!"

"I'll be right there!" Mr. McLean said.

As she watched him hurry to the telephone, Cindy decided that until he returned, she would have to be Glory's guardian. For now, watching him was all she could do.

6

SHINING WASN'T THE ONLY HORSE WITH A RACE COMING up. In less than two weeks, both she and Her Majesty would be racing in the Frizette at Belmont in New York, and Maddock had entered Townsend Princess in a two-year-old race there as well. Before all the horses were shipped north, Ashleigh, Samantha, and Cindy went to visit Townsend Acres to watch Princess's last training session at home.

The excitement around both farms was contagious, especially since all three fillies stood a good chance of performing well. "Of course, I won't exactly cry myself to sleep if Shining and I beat Her Majesty, as nice a horse as she is," Ashleigh joked, as they watched Lavinia's filly breeze out a fast eighth of a mile.

71

Fortunately, Princess's workout went well also, bolstering the Whitebrook crowd's spirits even more. Ashleigh was pleased with the filly's form, and she told Hank so. The groom had taken them back to the barn to see some of the Townsends' other promising horses.

"She's really been putting her heart into it lately, Ashleigh," Hank agreed. "No reason why she shouldn't tear up Belmont the way she tore up Saratoga."

"I hope so, Hank," Ashleigh said. "I've got a lot of dreams for her." While she and Samantha began to discuss the details of Princess's training, Cindy wandered around the barn, admiring the horses.

The only person who didn't seem to share the good humor was Lavinia. She had come into the barn to check on Her Majesty after the filly had been cooled out but had hurried off as soon as she saw the Whitebrook group, her bright red lips pursed unpleasantly.

Hank shook his head. "I hate to think what it will be like around here if Her Majesty loses to Shining again."

"You mean Lavinia could get worse than she already is? Impossible!" Samantha said.

Cindy started to giggle but stopped herself when she saw Lavinia herself returning to the barn. Her face set in an expression of rage, the woman stormed past them to Her Majesty's stall. She paused for a minute, then spun around, pointing a finger at Cindy. "I knew it! You're nothing but a thief!" she cried. "I knew you couldn't be trusted!"

Cindy gaped at Lavinia in disbelief.

"What are you talking about?" Samantha asked Lavinia sharply.

"That orphan stole my gold watch!" Lavinia shrieked.

"*What*?" Samantha asked incredulously.

"I left my gold watch on the bench outside Her Majesty's stall a few minutes ago. It's pure gold—a Swiss watch! Do you know how much a watch like that is worth? I just remembered it, came back to get it, and now it's gone!" Lavinia wailed. "And we all know who's desperate enough to take it! Hand it over or I'm reporting you to the police!"

Cindy's face had paled at the accusation. "I didn't take your watch. I swear it. I've never even seen it," she said, a sense of dread coming over her.

"Did you see her take it?" Ashleigh demanded.

"No, but it's obvious she did. Look at her background! A runaway! One foster home after another—and she was wandering around here all by herself while you three were talking. She had plenty of opportunity!"

"Calm down, Lavinia," Samantha said curtly. "You can't go around accusing people without any proof."

"I didn't take it!" Cindy said, turning desperately to Samantha and Ashleigh for support. She emptied out her pockets frantically.

"I believe you," Samantha said.

"So do I," Ashleigh said.

"Well, I don't! Wait till Brad hears about this!" Lavinia threatened. She turned to Cindy. "You'll have the police on your trail, you little thief! I'm sure the authorities will be interested to hear what you're learning at your new foster home!"

"That's enough!" Ashleigh cried, but Lavinia had already stormed off.

Cindy stared after her in shocked disbelief, unable to make sense of what had just happened. It was as if she had been plunged back into her former life. She felt the same blind terror she had when she'd been caught shoplifting—only this time she hadn't done anything.

Putting an arm around Cindy's shoulders, Samantha tried to comfort her while Ashleigh ran to get the Jeep. "Don't worry, Cindy. We're going to tell Mom and Dad right away. There's nothing Lavinia can do to hurt you. I *know* you didn't take it."

Cindy tried to listen to what Samantha was saying, but her thoughts were a panicked jumble. As soon as Lavinia called the police, she would find out about the previous trouble she'd gotten into for shoplifting. Then even the McLeans might begin to doubt her. All she could see was the authorities coming to Whitebrook as they had before—but now it would be to take her away for good.

When they got back to the farm, Cindy ran upstairs to her room and flung herself on her bed. She had cried herself out on the way home; now all she felt was cold dread. A few minutes later, the McLeans knocked on her door.

"Cindy? Samantha told us what happened," Beth began tentatively.

Cindy sat up in bed but said nothing.

"We're very angry at Lavinia's behavior," Mr. McLean said. "We're going to talk to her and Brad and straighten this thing out right away."

Beth picked up Cindy's hand and gave it a squeeze. "Don't worry, dear. I'm sure it's all a big misunderstanding. Try to cheer up, all right?"

Cindy nodded. She still didn't trust herself to speak. She was afraid whatever she said would make her sound guilty.

Her foster father looked at her anxiously before going on. "I do have to tell you that Lavinia has found out about your previous shoplifting, and she's going to try to use that against you."

Cindy looked up, mute with embarrassment.

"We've always known, Cindy," Beth said. "When we became your official foster parents, we were notified of your past record."

Cindy wasn't surprised. She knew they had known, but they had been kind enough not to bring it up and to trust her anyway, despite her past mistakes. But would they believe that she was innocent now?

"We're not going to badger you about this now. I just wanted to let you know what was going on," Mr. McLean concluded. "We'll try to help you fight this, honey."

Cindy nodded again, holding back tears. When the McLeans left, she lay back on her bed and stared up at the ceiling, praying that they would convince Lavinia of her innocence. But, she wondered, did they really believe it themselves? Would anyone?

The day, which had begun so perfectly was turning into her worst nightmare, and it only got worse. A few hours later, Cindy glimpsed a police car pulling up outside the house. She was summoned downstairs to talk with the juvenile officer. The McLeans all gave her encouraging smiles, but Cindy was too nervous to return them.

"Cindy, this officer just wants to ask you a few questions. It's nothing to worry about—just routine," Ian explained.

Cindy stared at the ground while the officer began his questioning. First he asked her general questions about how she liked living at Whitebrook and whether she felt that she had everything she needed.

"And if you ever wanted anything that wasn't yours, what would you do?" the officer asked.

"Listen, take it easy on her, all right?" Ian said tersely. "That's a pretty loaded question."

The officer took a deep breath. "Okay. Forget that one. It's not important. Now, let's see . . . " He paused to consult his notes. "I've talked to the child welfare people, and I know that you've had some, well, problems in the past, and I—"

"I didn't take her watch! I didn't! I swear I didn't!" Cindy cried, jumping to her feet.

Once again Mr. McLean interrupted. "Lavinia Townsend has absolutely no right to accuse Cindy," he said angrily.

"I realize that, sir, but the watch did disappear in the child's presence, and we have to investigate the matter. I'll go now, but I can't drop this case," the officer said firmly.

With that, Mr. McLean showed him immediately to the door. Cindy had thought that she didn't have another tear left, but she dissolved into tears as soon as the man had gone and began to tremble uncontrollably.

Samantha wrapped her arms around her, letting her cry.

"They're going to take me away," Cindy said tearfully. "I knew things were too good to be true. I've been so happy, but I guess I'm just not supposed to be."

All three McLeans tried to comfort her, but Cindy saw the worried looks on their faces and only cried harder.

She was inconsolable. She lay miserably on her bed the rest of the day, her arms around her tear-stained pillow. In one day, her whole happy new world was breaking into little pieces. She had feared this happening. She had dreaded it. But she hadn't thought it would occur over something she hadn't even done. The saddest part was that once she would have been capable of taking the watch. Thanks to the McLeans' taking her in and caring for her, she would rather die than disappoint them by stealing. But how could she possibly convince people who knew about her past that she had changed?

At dinner that evening nobody seemed to have anything to talk about. Beth had made her famous vegetable lasagna, but it tasted like lead in Cindy's mouth. After a few bites, she set her fork down.

"Cindy, we talked to the Townsends this afternoon," Mr. McLean said finally, when the subject could be avoided no longer. "I'll be honest with you. Lavinia is adamant in her accusations, and she refuses to withdraw the charges." He paused, looking at Cindy.

"Cindy," Beth finished for him, "if you know anything at all about the missing watch, it would be better to tell us now rather than wait until things get worse."

"We aren't accusing you, and we believe everything you've told us. We just don't want you to get hurt, honey," her foster father explained.

Cindy could hardly speak. All of a sudden, it sounded like the McLeans might not completely believe her. They seemed nervous—almost as if they were worried she was hiding something that the authorities would find out later. "I didn't take it. I didn't take the watch," she repeated in a near-whisper. "I don't know what it looks like. I've never seen it. I never wanted it." She stopped, unable to go on.

"How about some more lasagna, Beth?" Samantha asked in a determinedly cheerful voice, glancing at Cindy quickly.

"May I be excused?" Cindy asked. She just couldn't bear to sit at the table any longer.

"Go ahead," Beth said quietly, but Cindy had already fled the dining room.

That night Cindy felt more alone than she had felt since she had arrived at Whitebrook. She listened to the clatter of the dishes and wished she could go back downstairs and pretend nothing had happened. If only the McLeans had been her real parents! Then she'd be safe and protected forever. Instead, she was on the verge of losing everything she loved. Her final thought before she fell into a troubled sleep was that the happiest times she had known were coming to an end.

The next morning, a Sunday, Cindy felt slightly better. She would just have to wait and see what happened and defend herself when it did. It was a sunny, fall day, and, although the previous day's events nagged at her, she couldn't help enjoying the horses as always. She had a wistful thought that maybe the whole thing would blow over somehow, but she couldn't really believe it would.

After doing her morning chores, Cindy went to watch Samantha give Shining her final workout before the Beldame. The filly's training had been stepped up in anticipation of the coming race. Samantha galloped her through three-quarters of a mile, then breezed her out the last quarter. As she asked for the increased speed, Samantha leaned lower over Shining's neck. Cindy could see the filly flatten out and reach for the bit, her black mane flying, her legs a blur.

At the mile post, Samantha stood up in her stirrups. Shining slowed to a canter, and then a trot, and Samantha jogged her back along the rail for a quick consultation with her father. The filly came off the track tossing her head and barely winded.

For an instant, Cindy could forget her own problems. Her face was glowing with pride as she greeted horse and rider. She couldn't help but feel the tiniest bit responsible for Shining's great condition after all the hours she'd put in grooming and fussing over her. She reached up to give the roan neck a pat, then stopped dead in her tracks. Further down the rail, Brad and Lavinia stood watching the workouts. All the color drained from Cindy's face.

Samantha turned in the saddle, following her glance. When she saw the two of them, her face tightened in anger. "She's got some nerve coming over here after what she's done to you. Here," she said, hopping neatly to the ground. "Go cool out Shining. I've got a few things I'd like to say to Lavinia."

Cindy took Shining's reins gratefully. She wanted to get out of Lavinia's sight as soon as possible. In the

81

barn, she reached up to remove Shining's saddle and realized that her hands were shaking. She took several deep breaths before leading Shining out to one of the grassy paddock lanes to walk her.

"Oh, Shining, what'll I do?" she asked. The filly flicked her ears back as if to listen. "I'm so frightened they're going to take me away, and I'll never see you or any of the other horses again. It's not fair! Why should the authorities believe Lavinia? She has no proof! I'd miss you so much, Shining—I'd miss everyone here." Cindy paused to sniff back tears. Shining turned and gently butted her nose against Cindy's shoulder.

"Listen, Shining, I won't let them take me away. I'll run away first," Cindy vowed. Running away from Whitebrook hadn't occurred to her in a long time. Once she had settled in on the farm, she had even dared to hope it might become her permanent home. But Lavinia's accusation had put her right back on shaky ground. Running away would be a desperate measure, but if the authorities threatened to take her away, it would be her only choice.

7

CINDY COULD BARELY CONCENTRATE ON HER CLASSES AT school the next day. It was always a little hard to get back into it on Monday, but today was different. Math and English flew by in a blur. In French she got called on and couldn't remember a simple response. The French teacher, who had a silly sense of humor, teased her for the rest of class about her forgetfulness. When she finally escaped to lunch, Cindy was in a deeper funk than before.

"All right, Cindy, come clean," Heather said as the girls walked together to the cafeteria. "What on earth is bothering you? You stared out the window during French class, and you barely even said hello to me."

Startled, Cindy glanced sharply at Heather. "Oh,

Heather, I'm sorry. I can't concentrate on anything," Cindy said.

"That much is obvious," Heather replied kiddingly. "What's wrong?"

Cindy chewed on her lip for a minute. She wanted nothing more than to talk about her problem with Heather. But something stopped her. What if Heather thought she had taken the watch, too? Then she would lose all respect for Cindy and probably wouldn't want to be friends anymore.

"Cindy," Heather said gently, "you can tell me."

At the concerned look on Heather's face, Cindy made an instant decision to explain. Choking back tears, she related the whole story in a rush. It was particularly hard to tell the part about her past. She was so afraid her friend would really think she was a thief. "I did try to steal once, but I would never, ever take anything again."

During the account, Heather's lips had narrowed into a thin line, and her blue eyes flashed angrily. "But how could Lavinia do that to you?" she demanded. "It's totally unfair!"

Cindy sighed. She felt calmer having shared her problem with Heather. "You don't know Lavinia Townsend. Sammy and Ashleigh have told me all kinds of horrible things she's done. If she doesn't like someone, she'll do anything to get them out of her way."

*   *   *

After school, Beth told Cindy that the best thing she could do to stop thinking about the situation would be to keep as busy as possible. At Whitebrook, that wasn't hard to do. Samantha, Ashleigh, and Mike were leaving at five a.m. the next morning for New York. They were taking Shining and two of Mike's horses and would be gone five days. Before they left, there was the usual flurry of pre-race activity, and Cindy threw herself into things wholeheartedly. She helped organize tack, blankets, brushes, and buckets with Samantha. She rolled bandages, measured feed, and swept out the horse van. The next morning, she was up at dawn to see the group off and help with all the extra chores.

Everyone was optimistic about Shining's chances in the Beldame. Before Samantha loaded the filly into the van, Cindy gave Shining a good-luck hug. "Do you think she needs the good luck, Sammy?" she asked.

Samantha laughed. "All horses and all owners and all trainers and all jockeys always need good luck. So much can happen in a race. And as you know, Shining will be facing Her Majesty again."

"You can beat her," Cindy said solemnly. "But here's good luck for you, too." As she spoke, Cindy hugged Samantha good-bye.

85

"Keep your chin up, Cindy," Samantha whispered. "Everything is going to work out." Then she turned and led Shining up the ramp of the van.

Cindy waited while the other horses were loaded. She watched the van rumble up the driveway. Then she squared her shoulders determinedly. There was work to be done.

Over the next couple of days, Cindy tried to do what Samantha had said and look on the bright side, but it was hard. The McLeans hadn't heard anything from the police or the child welfare people, and, with Samantha and Shining gone, Cindy felt lonely. The house and the racing barn seemed strangely deserted. She was glad when her foster father offered to ride out and visit Glory on Wednesday afternoon. To Cindy's disappointment, when they reached the neighboring property, the field was totally empty. At first, she could hardly believe it. "Every time before, the horse has been here," she said, disconcerted. It made her nervous to think of the men taking Glory away, even if it was only up to the stable.

"Still, it's not surprising he would be gone once in a while," Mr. McLean pointed out gently. "The owners could be grooming him, riding him, keeping him inside—anything."

Cindy realized that her foster father's words made sense, but she was discouraged nonetheless. "I have the feeling that whatever they're doing with him can't be good," she said.

"You may be right, and I'm sorry I didn't get a chance to see the horse," Mr. McLean said, turning his mount toward home. "We'll have to come back out, that's all there is to it. I won't be able to get the time until the end of next week, though. I've got business meetings almost every afternoon." He paused, looking at Cindy's crestfallen expression. "I'm sorry—I'd like to check out this situation for myself, and believe me, I will. In the meantime, let me know if you see those men again, okay?"

Cindy nodded glumly. Her foster father was doing the best he could to help her. She knew what it meant for him to take an hour to make the trip on horseback: by the time they got back, he would have a stack of messages on his desk, all of which would need his attention right away. She would have to continue to watch out for Glory herself.

To try to cheer herself up, Cindy invited Heather over near the end of the week. They planned to help with the halter breaking of the twin orphan foals and then go for a trail ride, checking on Glory along the way.

Since Ian McLean was busy, Vic and Len had the

two foals haltered when the girls arrived at the stable. The little colts were used to wearing the halters. What they hadn't learned yet was how to behave properly at the end of a lead line. Most foals simply followed their mothers to and from the pasture for the first few months. But since these foals' mother had died at birth, they had been handled by people more than most foals their age. Still, whoever turned them out usually just looped a leadline around their necks or guided them by hand. Now they had to learn to walk beside their handlers and to halt when asked. It was important to do this basic training early, when the foals were still small and responsive. Otherwise, they could turn into headstrong yearlings who plowed past trainers and grooms.

Len grinned when he saw Cindy and Heather. The stable manager had taken a fancy to both Cindy, for her quiet ways around the horses, and her calm, level-headed friend. "Why don't you girls each take a foal?" he suggested.

"Really, Len?" Cindy asked, but the older man was already pressing a lead line into her hands.

"Here you go. Snap it right to his halter. You're going to lead him out of the barn as if you did it every day. After all, this shouldn't be a big deal. Same for you, Heather."

When they were ready to go, Cindy and Heather

led the foals forward. They followed obediently, accustomed as they were to walking alongside humans. When they got to the end of the aisle, however, Heather's foal dug his heels in, not wanting to leave the stable. She pulled on his leadline, urging him forward.

"You'll never get anywhere like that," Vic commented with a chuckle.

Heather smiled wryly. "All right. How do I get him to move?"

"You've got to encourage him from behind. You can never turn around, stare a horse in the face, and pull him forward—it just won't work," Vic explained. "Instead, stand back by his shoulder and give a little flick with the end of the lead shank."

Heather tried Vic's suggestion. Not surprisingly, it worked. The foal obeyed the gentle tap on his flank from the lead line and walked forward again. Up ahead, Cindy turned around and gave her the thumbs-up sign. Len and Vic walked beside the two of them, helping them as they took the foals back and forth along the path that led to the weanlings' pasture. Cindy couldn't remember the last time she had had so much fun. She always loved working with the foals, and having Heather along to do something important in the training made it an even bigger treat.

"Now if only I could think up names!" she called to the others, her high spirits bubbling over.

After the training session, the girls decided to check on Glory. Cindy had filled Heather in on her disappointing trip out to the paddock with her foster father. Heather was eager to go out to see the horse, too.

"At least we can let him know that we're his friends—and not everyone is mean and nasty," Cindy said, as they trotted along the trail an hour later. She tried to make her voice sound more hopeful than she felt. At least until her foster father saw the horse, poor Glory was just one more thing in her life that she had no control over.

"That's right," Heather agreed. "And someday we may be able to help him—someday soon, I'll bet."

If I'm still here, Cindy thought, shivering.

To the girls' delight, Glory was alone in his paddock. They stopped Bo Jangles and Chips at the trailhead and listened for the sound of voices, but there were none. Just to be safe, they tied the horses at the edge of the woods so that they would be hidden if anyone approached. Then they crept forward to the fence.

"Come on, boy. Come say hi," Cindy murmured. She and Heather held out the carrots they had brought with them. At first, the horse stayed where he was, watching the girls warily. He pricked his ears at the sound of their voices and seemed to want to come forward. After a few minutes of coaxing, they dropped their carrots inside the fence and stepped away. Finally, the horse approached the wall. He walked slowly, not letting his guard down, snatched the carrots up, and then retreated a few paces.

"He's much more scared now than when I first saw him," Cindy said miserably. "He used to like people. Those men have really done a job on him. If only my foster father could have seen him—I'm sure he would have realized something was wrong."

Heather gazed at the horse compassionately. "I can't stand how afraid he looks. He's so beautiful. I don't understand how such a terrible owner could have gotten him."

"Neither do I," Cindy said. "He looks like he should be in a palace of a barn and have ten grooms all to himself—not stuck out in this pasture."

They watched the horse for a while longer. Then Cindy moved toward the paddock fence. She spoke in a low voice. "I don't know your name, boy, but I call you 'Glory.' We're your friends, and we care about what happens to you. We can't take you away from those awful men, but we'll be back as often as we can. Okay?"

The gray colt looked at them. His large, dark eyes

seemed to plead with them. He nickered softly as if he understood what Cindy had said.

Cindy was determined to find out more about the new owner of the farm. The more she thought about her conversation with Heather, the more frustrated Cindy felt. Why was the horse there in the field, anyway? And why hadn't Mr. McLean been able to find out anything about the neighbors? There was only one way to find out—go to the farm herself. It was risky, but it might give her some answers.

After school the next day Cindy got out an old bike of Samantha's that the McLeans had given her to use and pedaled down the driveway to the road. She hoped no one would see her leaving and ask where she was heading. Looking behind her every few minutes, she quickly pedaled along the road to the front of the neighbor's fenced property a mile away.

She felt a wave of disappointment when she stopped the bike and looked in. A chain-link fence ran the length of the property. It was overgrown with vines which blocked the view, and it made pretending to take a walk or casually riding onto the land impossible. The big gates which crossed the driveway were locked with a heavy padlock. Through the gates Cindy could glimpse the house and barn, but just barely. They sat well back from the road and were surrounded by trees and overgrown shrubbery. The leaves on the scraggly lawn hadn't been raked and blew aimlessly. Except for a pickup truck parked by the barn, Cindy would have guessed the place was deserted. It certainly looked nothing like the active racing barns or breeding facilities she had seen. Discouraged, Cindy took a last look around before riding home. She found that she was pedaling faster than before. Something about the place gave her the creeps.

All afternoon, while she helped Vic turn out the mares and give Precocious and Mr. Wonderful a good grooming, Cindy thought about Glory. She was scared of his owners, but she kept thinking of him all alone in the pasture. "He needs friends even more than I do," she told herself, and, knowing that, she found the courage to go and visit him.

She decided to walk out so that she wouldn't have to worry about the men noticing a horse. It took a long time on foot. Finally Cindy reached the end of Whitebrook property. She watched for a minute, saw no sign of the men, then ran down to the paddock fence, eager to see Glory. This time, the horse seemed happy to see her. As a special treat, Cindy had brought sugar lumps, as well as the usual carrots. Glory came forward and ate them from her hand, allowing her to stroke his neck. She spoke gently to him as she did. She could see that the big horse was gradually relaxing, deciding this new friend was someone he could trust. He took a step closer and leaned his head out further over the top of the fence. He whuffed softly as Cindy reached up to scratch his ears.

Cindy slipped into a daydream in which she was Glory's owner, and she rode him all the time. "You'd have a huge stall in the training barn, and Ashleigh and Samantha and Tor would coach us . . . " Cindy's voice trailed off dreamily.

Too late, she realized her mistake. While she had been dreaming, the two men had appeared at the other side of the paddock. Cindy sensed their presence when Glory suddenly flung up his head and shied away from her. Before she could run, the older man saw her. He came charging in her direction, brandishing a long, coiled longe whip which he slapped against his hand.

"You there! You're trespassing! Get off my property, and don't come back if you know what's good for you!"

Cindy raced away from him, up the hill to Whitebrook's land. She felt her jeans rip when they caught on the branch of a gnarled old bush. Her heart was pounding furiously as she raced for the woods. When she could safely hide herself behind a tree, she peeked around cautiously to see what was going on.

Glory had retreated in fear from the man who had chased Cindy, but, as she watched, the son grabbed his halter. The older man tried to put the saddle on his back, but Glory reared, backing away as fast as he could. With the butt end of his whip, the man gave him a vicious knock between the ears. "Behave yourself, you brute," he yelled.

Cindy felt sick to her stomach, and cold with anger and fear. She simply had to do something—but what?

8

THE STABLES WERE ABUZZ WITH EXCITEMENT THE NEXT morning. It was Saturday—Shining's race day at Belmont. Post-time for the Grade 1 Beldame Stakes was four P.M. At three-thirty sharp, an enthusiastic crowd had gathered in the McLeans' family room to watch the pre-race activities on television. Looking around the room, Cindy felt the familiar feeling of warmth that seemed to pervade all gatherings at Whitebrook. The McLeans had invited Tor and Heather to come over and watch the race with them. Heather, who was ensconsed happily in Ian McLean's overstuffed armchair, looked delighted to be included in the Whitebrook circle. She had her drawing pad open and was sketching the mares and fillies entered in the Beldame.

"Come on, honey! Sammy's got Shining tacked up and is bringing her out into the walking ring!" Mr. McLean called.

Beth appeared in the doorway, carrying a plate of chips and salsa. "Have the jockeys come into the ring yet?" she asked anxiously.

"No, but there's a good shot of Sammy leading Shining around the ring."

Beth squeezed in between her husband and Tor. Beth had told Cindy that she hadn't known the first thing about racing a year ago. Since meeting Mr. McLean, she had become well-versed in track terminology and never missed a Whitebrook race. When Shining appeared on the screen again, led by Samantha, Cindy saw Beth clasp her husband's hand excitedly.

Cindy smiled. She was incredibly excited, too, and had inched forward on her chair until she was perched on the very edge, her eyes glued to the screen. It had been amazing to watch Samantha and Ashleigh in action at Saratoga, but seeing them on TV was thrilling in an entirely different way. She grinned with pride when the TV announcer, who was standing beside the walking ring, recounted Shining's rags-to-riches story.

"Leading the co-favorite in the race today is her owner, Samantha McLean, the girl who nursed the filly back to health. Hard to believe this fit and handsome filly was racing in the claiming ranks at second-rate tracks just a year ago. She's come a long way. Then again, maybe that's not surprising for a half sister to the incredible race mare and Derby winner, Ashleigh's Wonder." The cameras focussed on Samantha and Shining. In contrast to two of the other fillies who were acting up, Shining looked interested in the scene yet relaxed.

Her walk alone was a magnificent testament to her breeding and speed. She covered the ground with the grace of a cat, her muscles rippling in the sun. Walking at her side, Samantha beamed from ear-to-ear. Her red hair was set off dramatically by Shining's unusual red roan coat. Cindy stole a quick glance at Tor. He looked a million miles away with an expression of pure love and admiration on his face.

"They're quite a pair, aren't they?" he sighed, half to himself.

A few minutes later, the jockeys appeared. Ashleigh looked neat and workmanlike in the Whitebrook blue-and-white silks. Samantha gave her a leg up into Shining's saddle. Mike joined the two of them in the ring, and they all began to discuss strategy. Since Samantha wasn't a licensed trainer, Mike stood in as the official trainer. The camera continued to scan the rest of the field in the Beldame, as the announcer gave some background on each. The camera came to rest on Her Majesty.

"And here's the other favorite in the race," the announcer began, "owned by Lavinia Townsend of Townsend Acres . . . " It irked Cindy to see that the bay filly looked wonderful, as did her owner. Sensing the camera on her, Lavinia smiled prettily at Brad who stood by her side. As always, the two of them made a handsome couple. Lavinia was wearing a dark suit which showed off her perfect complexion. Obviously, she had spent hours at the beauty parlor: her blond hair was elaborately curled and piled on her head.

It infuriated Cindy more to see the flash of a diamond watch band on Lavinia's wrist. *How could she get so upset over losing one watch when she had another, probably more expensive one, at home?* Cindy wondered, her stomach clenching in anger. She could sense her foster parents casting worried looks her way and tried to put Lavinia out of her mind.

But fifteen minutes later, when the starting gates flew open and twelve magnificent Thoroughbred fillies surged out onto the track, Cindy no longer had to try. It was impossible to concentrate on anything but Shining and Ashleigh. From start to finish, Shining put in a brilliant performance, and Ashleigh gave her a textbook-perfect ride. Breaking cleanly from their number three post position, the pair stayed behind the leaders and just off the pace for the first half of the mile and an eighth race. Her Majesty uncharacteristically hung back mid-pack, and instead of making a move on the far turn, the bay filly looked like she was laboring.

Entering the stretch, Ashleigh waited for a hole on the inside, shot Shining through on the rail, and asked her to turn on the speed. Shining hardly needed to be asked. She sprang forward, pulling even with a dark chestnut mare.

"That's Pretty Peggy! She's a four-year-old who's notched up tons of stakes victories. . . . Do you think Shining can—" Tor stopped suddenly as Shining made his question unnecessary.

In a sizzling drive, she passed the mare, lengthened her lead to three strides and won going away. Cindy, Heather, Tor, and the McLeans sprang to their feet cheering and hugging one another, as the unofficial results flashed across the screen. Pretty Peggy finished second, followed by a longshot in third. Her Majesty had crossed the line a lackluster sixth.

"Look at them! They're being mobbed!" Mr. McLean exclaimed, a proud smile nearly splitting his face. As Samantha approached the winner's circle, leading Shining and Ashleigh, a crowd of racing reporters surrounded the three of them, snapping pictures and shouting questions. The TV anchor muscled his way forward. He congratulated Ashleigh on her ride, then shook hands with Samantha. "Can you tell me, Miss McLean, what you did to turn this horse around—a horse who, a year ago, was racing in the lowest claiming ranks?" he asked.

Samantha rubbed Shining's forehead affectionately. "I just gave her care and love," she responded. "She did the rest."

The camera shot suddenly switched to a view of LeBlanc, Her Majesty's jockey, who looked tired and disappointed. One of the network commentators had a microphone pushed up toward his face and was asking him what went wrong with Her Majesty.

"I don't know," Le Blanc said in a weary tone. "She broke clean, but coming down the backstretch I knew she wasn't digging in. She didn't seem to like the track. She wouldn't kick in when I asked her." Le Blanc shook his head. "I don't want to make excuses for her, but today wasn't her day."

The jockey turned his head away, and Cindy actually felt sorry for him and Her Majesty. Who could know why Her Majesty didn't fire? Being a co-favorite and coming in sixth had to be humiliating. Cindy couldn't direct her anger toward the horse and jockey, even when the horse's owner was Lavinia Townsend.

After watching the post-race presentation, the elated group turned off the TV and discussed the victory before going their separate ways.

As soon as Heather left for home, Cindy's thoughts turned once again to Glory. She hadn't said anything to her foster parents about getting caught on the neighbors' property. She was in enough trouble as it was, and she knew that any wrongdoing—even if it was completely unrelated to the watch incident—would be held against her by the authorities. If they suspected she was lying and stealing while living with the McLeans, they would insist on taking her away for sure. So far, nobody from Child Protection had come out to the farm to investigate, but Cindy guessed it was only a matter of time.

She knew she should bring up the incident with the McLeans, but she was afraid that even *they* would associate her tresspassing with general dishonesty. She couldn't bear for them to doubt her innocence. Still, she felt both afraid that they would find out, and guilty that she hadn't told them. Every time the phone rang, she jumped, thinking it was the man calling to tell her foster parents that she'd been caught on his property.

But even though Cindy knew that going back to visit Glory put her at risk, she simply couldn't give up on him. She was his only friend. He needed her.

That thought alone gave her the courage to go to him.

Cindy told the McLeans she was going to take a walk before dinner.

"Do you want company, honey?" Beth asked kindly.

"No, thanks. I just want to do some thinking on my own," Cindy replied, praying that her voice sounded casual.

"I understand. Sometimes you need to mull things over alone," Beth said sympathetically. "So we'll see you for dinner at around six."

Cindy nodded and turned away, not trusting herself to speak. She longed to ask Beth to come with her, but this was a problem she had to deal with alone.

Before heading to the neighbor's farm, she stopped by the storeroom in the barn and filled her jacket pockets with carrots. Then she set out on foot, hoping to find Glory alone. The beautiful trail held no pleasure for Cindy that afternoon. She hurried along without seeing anything, her hands sweaty with nerves and her heart pounding. She had decided not to risk going down to the pasture again but instead planned to stay hidden and toss the carrots over the fence. "I'm coming, Glory," she repeated to herself. "Don't worry, boy, I'm coming."

But when she got to the edge of the woods

overlooking the field, she stopped short: Glory wasn't there. Completely forgetting the danger, Cindy ran to the fence and scanned the pasture desperately for signs of the horse. At the sight of the empty field, she felt her heart sink to her feet. Had they taken him away for good? Why, oh why, Cindy asked herself, hadn't she done something before? "I *should* have stolen him! At least then one of us would be happy, and I'd get blamed for something I actually did!" she cried bitterly.

Feeling leaden, she turned and headed back down the trail toward Whitebrook at a run. At the thought of the men's cruelty toward Glory, her anger at the unfairness of life bubbled over. She started to run, pounding down the trail. Just like Glory, she'd been raised with no love—forced into homes where she didn't want to be—and now it could happen again, to both of them. All she could think about was how wrong it was that Glory was in the hands of the wrong people, too. She ran until she was completely spent and out of breath. Gasping, she came out of the woods and skirted its edge, going along the far side of the Whitebrook pastures.

As she walked along wearily, she thought she heard a noise to her right. Whatever it was sounded almost like the snort of a horse, but she knew Mike's horses wouldn't be running loose. She stopped to listen. Again she heard a soft snort, this time followed by the rustle of dry leaves. She took a few steps closer and peered through the now sparse, autumn-tinted leaves. Her heart skipped a beat as she saw a flicker of gray and then heard a nicker.

"Glory! Oh, Glory! You're here!" Cindy breathed. "I wish you could talk and tell me how you got here, Glory. I'll bet you jumped out of the pasture. The question is: do the men know you're gone? And what on earth am I going to do with you?"

In spite of her delight at finding the horse, Cindy knew she had to act fast. Glory's owners would no doubt be on the lookout for him soon if they weren't already. There was no question in her mind about returning him to them, but what could she do with him? Where could she put him? The obvious answer was to take him to Whitebrook, but she knew that Mike and her foster father would then have no choice but to contact the owners. Then Cindy remembered something. There was a small storage shed to the rear of the paddocks. It was used for storing extra hay and shavings and some farm equipment. She could hide Glory there while she figured out what to do. He would be safe and out of sight. There was a water supply nearby for filling the troughs in the rear paddocks, and she could easily slip him some grain without anyone finding out. For an instant, Cindy thought about the consequences of hiding the beautiful colt. But then she remembered the night she had run away from her old foster parents, ending up asleep in a stall at Whitebrook. Her decision was made. She couldn't let Glory down.

"Easy does it, boy. It's only me. Don't be afraid." Cindy talked softly to the horse, taking a carrot from her pocket and holding it out on the palm of her hand. Slowly she approached the gray colt. He stayed where he was, his eyes watching her, his ears pricked forward. Cindy edged herself closer as quietly as she could, knowing that if anything startled him, he could bolt, and she could lose him forever.

But Glory stood his ground. When he smelled the treat, his nostrils flared, and he stretched forward to lip up the carrot. Cindy quickly took a hold of his halter. The minute she caught him, Glory started in alarm, but Cindy kept talking soothingly to him. She rubbed the gray neck gently. "You remember me. I'm your friend, and I'm going to help you. I know how you feel because I ran away once, too. And you know what? We both picked the right place."

As Glory began to relax, Cindy fed him another carrot. Then she coaxed him forward out of the wood, leading him along its edge toward the storage shed. Dusk was falling. Cindy knew she would probably be late for dinner, but it was too late to turn back now.

She would just have to think of an excuse. She was less worried about the McLeans being angry than she was that the nasty neighbor would suddenly burst out of the woods and catch her taking his horse away. If that happened, she would really be in big trouble.

By the time they reached the shed, Cindy's heart was pounding nervously. Every creak of a branch sounded like approaching footsteps. Without wasting any time, she yanked off her belt and used it to tie Glory to the outside of the shed. She had to keep him safe while she set up his stall. Working as fast as she could, she moved all of the tools in the shed to one side, blocking them off with bales of hay. She opened a bale of sweet-smelling straw and spread it on the floor. Then she tossed some loose hay into the "stall" and filled a bucket with water from the tap outside. The setup wasn't perfect, but it would have to do for now. When she led him in, Glory looked around a little uneasily, acquainting himself with his new surroundings. But what he saw and sniffed in the air seemed to reassure him. A moment later, he began munching hay, a good sign.

As he ate, Cindy looked him over carefully. He was thinner than he had been when she had first seen him, and his coat lacked the shine it had once had. But what made Cindy gape in horror was a raw welt on the horse's flank. As she examined it more closely,

Cindy realized it was the result of a lashing whip. She got a cloth, dampened it at the spigot, and carefully cleaned out the wound. Glory flinched when she touched it, his eyes wide with pain.

"You poor thing," Cindy said. The welt, an unequivocal sign of abuse, made her more determined than ever that the horse should not be sent back to the neighbors. "No matter what happens, I won't let them take you," she whispered. Glory looked at her calmly. Then he reached his head forward and gently touched his velvet nose to her chest, as if he knew he wouldn't be mistreated here.

Cindy hated to leave him to go back to the cottage for dinner. He might get lonely all alone. "I know what I'll do," she said aloud. "I'll bring you a kitten to keep you company. How about that?" There were tons of cats around the barn, and those cats always seemed to be having kittens. One probably wouldn't be missed for awhile.

Cindy slipped out the door of the shed, took one long glance back at Glory, and ran.

9

THE ALARM CLOCK BUZZED LOUDLY, JARRING CINDY awake. She groaned, slapped the snooze button, and turned over. Funny, she thought, laying her head back on the pillow, it seemed even darker than usual. Then all at once she sat bolt upright in bed. It was darker because it was earlier: four in the morning, to be precise. The events of the night before came rushing back to her. After leaving Glory, she had run back for dinner, nearly an hour late. Fortunately, the McLeans had started eating without her. Cindy had apologized profusely and said that she had wandered off farther than she realized.

Beth had waved off her apology, and the rest of the dinner conversation had centered on Shining's victory, which everyone was still ecstatic about.

109

Straight after dinner, Cindy had gone up to her room. She was sure that her guilty secret was written all over her face.

Now, shaking off sleep with a superhuman effort, Cindy rose and dressed. Even her foster father didn't get up until around five, and the house was completely still. She grabbed an apple to munch on and slipped out the front door silently.

Her first stop was the tack room in the training barn. She grabbed a few brushes from a crate of extras, a lead line, a light cotton blanket, and some ointment for treating cuts. She put this into a bucket, along with as much sweet feed from the feed room as she could carry. As she was leaving, she heard a plaintive "meow" behind her.

"Thank you for reminding me, Jeeves," Cindy said, smiling down at the black-and-white stable tomcat. She set her bucket down and went to look in the stable office. The cats liked to sleep in the office because it was warm. This morning there were three half-grown kittens curled up on a blanket. Cindy found a basket and, after a few moments' anxious debate with herself, she chose one whose fur was an unusual mix of gray and white. "You'll match Glory perfectly," Cindy told the kitten, plopping him gently into the basket with a bag of cat food. Then, armed with basket and bucket, she set out for the shed.

The moon and stars had disappeared, and Cindy struggled along slowly in the predawn darkness. When she reached the shed, she breathed a huge sigh of relief. Even though it was very early, Vic or Len might have been up and about and could have seen her. But she seemed to have made it all right. As she opened the door of the shed, a loud whinny greeted her. Cindy grinned at the welcoming sound. "So, you survived out here alone, huh, boy?" she asked cheerily, setting down her load.

As soon as the basket touched ground, the kitten squirmed out, mewing loudly. Cindy picked him up to show to Glory. "I brought a friend for you, boy," she said, holding the kitten up so he could see. In response, Glory gave a low nicker. The kitten stared at the big, gray head and dug his claws into Cindy's arms.

"Ow! You imp! Stop that!" Cindy pulled the kitten from her shoulder and dumped him unceremoniously to the ground where he began to fight playfully with the straw.

"Trust me—he'll be great company," Cindy said to Glory. Without further delay, she sorted out the things she had brought and gave Glory his grain. The horse plunged his nose eagerly into the bucket she had hung up. While he ate, Cindy refilled his water bucket, gave him more hay and did some hasty mucking out. She didn't have time to give him a full grooming, but she cleaned the welt again and put some ointment on it. Before she left, she buckled the cotton blanket over the horse and shook out a dish of catfood for the kitten. "I'll be back as soon as I can," Cindy promised, giving Glory a final pat.

As she swung open the door to go, a shadowy shape sprang from a pile of straw and attacked her leg. Laughing, Cindy shook the kitten off. "You are an imp—and that's what I'm going to call you: Imp. Glory and Imp . . . it has a nice ring to it."

Dawn was beginning to break in the east as Cindy hurried back toward the farm buildings. She had never before witnessed the very early morning at Whitebrook. It awed her with its beauty. In spite of all her troubles, she felt a peaceful feeling steal over her for the few minutes that it took her to reach the mares' barn.

"Well, you're up early," Len said cheerily as she entered the barn.

Cindy smiled nervously. She couldn't help feeling a touch of panic. Had Len noticed something? Was his remark supposed to trick her into admitting something? "Uh, yeah—I couldn't sleep," Cindy said finally.

Len gave a brief nod, continuing down the aisle with the hose he used for watering. Cindy let out a breath of relief. At least nobody at Whitebrook seemed to suspect her yet. Her main worry remained the men who owned the horse. She was sure they must have discovered that he was gone and was equally sure that they would make an effort to get him back. If they came onto the property to look for him and found the shed—Cindy shuddered—it was too horrible to imagine.

After all of her chores were finished, which were increased with Ashleigh, Mike, and Samantha away, Cindy felt more on edge than ever. She kept thinking that Len, Vic, and her foster father were giving her strange looks. If they were, it was no surprise: in her preoccupied state of mind, she kept making silly mistakes. She had switched Fleet Goddess's and Wonder's grain and had had to switch them back, she had turned a yearling out in the wrong field, and she had forgotten to muck one of the stalls. Luckily, her foster father didn't seem to remember that the two of them were supposed to ride out again to try to check up on Glory. Cindy kept her mouth shut, praying that he wouldn't bring up the subject.

Going up to the house to get her Sunday breakfast, Cindy clenched and unclenched her hands. She simply had to confide in someone or she would go crazy. She thought about waiting until Monday when she would see Heather in school but decided she would invite her friend over to go riding that afternoon. If she couldn't come, she would simply have to get through one more day alone. "Some criminal I'd make," Cindy thought ruefully. "I'd be calling up everyone I knew to tell them where I'd hidden the jewels."

Fortunately, Heather could come over. She jumped at the chance to go riding and said her mother could drive her over after lunch. For the rest of the morning, Cindy cleaned her room from top to bottom. She had so much nervous energy that she couldn't sit still. When Heather knocked on the door, she ran down the stairs two at a time.

Despite her excitement, Cindy waited until they had set out on their ride to tell Heather about Glory. She was too scared to even mention his name around the barns for fear she would be overheard.

"So you found him in the woods?" Heather asked, trying to sort out Cindy's jumbled story.

"Right. And I took him to the storage shed at the back of the property. He seems to be doing okay."

"Anywhere's better than with those men," Heather said firmly. Cindy noticed the excited flush in her friend's cheeks. She suddenly felt like the two of them were sharing a huge adventure.

"That's what I was hoping you'd say!" Cindy cried. "I was so worried about, well, stealing him, but

I just couldn't return him to those awful, awful people."

"Of course not!" Heather exclaimed, looking horrified at the thought. "You saved that horse from being abused."

"It's just that now I don't really know what to do. Feeding him is going to be a huge problem. He's a big horse, and he's young, too. I'll bet he's still growing. You should see what Len gives the two-year-olds to eat—its unbelievable what they put away in a single day. I don't know how I'll be able to keep sneaking away grain without somebody noticing," Cindy said glumly.

Heather frowned, realizing the difficulties. "I still say you did the right thing," she said. "If there's anything I could do to help—"

"Thanks. It helps a lot just to have someone to talk to," Cindy replied.

"Have you thought about telling Samantha?" Heather suggested. "That welt you found is proof of abuse, right?"

"I think it is, but there's no way I want to tell Sammy. She'd have to tell her parents," Cindy explained. "The less they know, the better. With what's going on with Lavinia, I don't want them to have to hide things from the authorities."

When they got to the shed, Glory whinnied a

happy greeting. He had been pacing his improvised stall and seemed less relaxed than before. "I'll bet he's stir crazy in here," Cindy said. "It can't be easy to go from being out all of the time to being in all of the time, even if he's well cared for here."

The girls tied their mounts to the far side of the shed where they wouldn't be seen. Cindy snapped a lead line to Glory's halter and led him out. The horse bounded out eagerly, prancing along between the two of them. After a few minutes of silence, Heather voiced both of their thoughts. "It's not going to be easy to keep him exercised, either, is it?" she asked quietly.

"I know," Cindy said, sighing. "He needs a field to run around in. I can take him for walks, but it will be practically impossible to keep everyone at Whitebrook from finding out what's going on."

"What would you do if someone found out?" Heather asked in barely a whisper.

Cindy stopped Glory and looked at her friend. "If I get caught? I don't know. I'll bet everyone will think I'm a thief." She lowered her voice. "Sometimes I think about running away—with Glory—if I have to." Cindy waited to see how Heather would take her plan. She knew it was a desperate one, but she had to be ready in case the worst happened. To her relief, the pale girl nodded solemnly.

"If you run away, you have to tell me where you go," Heather said.

Cindy nodded. "Deal," she said.

Both girls were reluctant to leave Glory in the shed. Once he was back inside, they dawdled for almost an hour, currying and brushing his dappled grey coat until it shone in the dim light. Imp pounced over several times to see what they were up to, pausing to rub himself against Glory's legs.

"Boy, it didn't take him long to feel at home," Cindy remarked. She scooped up the kitten and held him against her cheek. "Why can't horses be as easy to take care of as cats?"

Heather laughed, happy to see that Cindy hadn't lost her sense of humor. "For the same reason cats aren't as much fun to ride as horses," she said.

They rode back to the barn slowly, going over Cindy's plan of action for the next couple of days. Heather promised to be "on call" and to come over in case of an emergency. "And if you think they're catching on, you have to promise to tell me right away," she added.

Cindy promised, too. When Heather left, Cindy felt bereft and scared again. Her evening chores went by in a blur. She raced out to feed Glory after dinner and, hardly stopping to pat him or talk to him, she ran back. All the way she thought she felt someone's eyes on her—the men, she thought—letting her imagination get the better of her. Maybe they'd guessed that she'd hidden their horse and would reach out and grab her in the darkness, drag her back to their farm, and lock her away until she told them where he was. She extended her stride to a flat out run until she reached the cottage.

When she was safely home, she watched television with her foster parents, escaping to her room as soon as she could.

"Feeling tired, Cindy?" her foster father asked as she headed up the stairs.

Cindy spun around on the steps, immediately on her guard, but Ian only looked concerned in a fatherly way. "Yeah—I'm really sleepy. I haven't been able to sleep too well lately."

"Is it the watch?" he asked.

Cindy nodded. "Too much on my mind, I guess." At least, she figured, that much was true.

10

ON MONDAY AFTERNOON, THE SCHOOL BUS STOPPED AT Whitebrook's driveway. Cindy fairly flew out the door. Ashleigh, Mike, and Samantha had been due to arrive back home while she was at school. She could hardly wait to congratulate them on their success. In addition to Shining's victory, one of Mike's young fillies had run a surprising second in the Frizette, a two-year-old race for fillies. The best news was that Townsend Princess had won it. Cindy knew she ought to feel as happy about Princess's success as she did about Shining's. After all, Ashleigh had a love for both horses and was half-owner of Princess, besides which, Princess was Wonder's daughter. But she couldn't seem to muster the same excitement about the chestnut filly's race. Anything connected with

Townsend Acres reminded her of Lavinia Townsend, a name which made her feel physically sick.

Cindy was also worried about Samantha's being back. As much as she wanted to see the older girl, Cindy knew it would be harder to sneak away to visit Glory. Ashleigh and Mike were usually too preoccupied to notice things that they weren't immediately concerned with, but Samantha lived in the same house as Cindy and often ended up in the barn at the same times she did. Cindy knew she was going to have to be extra careful about accounting for her whereabouts. She just couldn't put Samantha in the position of having to keep a secret from her parents for Cindy's sake.

Inside the racing barn, Ashleigh was avidly recounting the Beldame race to Len, Mr. McLean, and Mr. Reese. Samantha and Mike stood nearby, chiming in every so often with more details. "You're back!" Cindy cried, rushing down the aisle. She hugged each of them in turn.

"Yup, we're back. We had a little van trouble in Pennsylvania, but nothing my wife the mechanic couldn't take care of," Mike replied, beaming at Ashleigh.

"So how's Shining?" she asked eagerly. "Did she come out of the race okay?"

"You're just like us," Samantha said. "You always

want to know about the horses first and the people second." Grinning, she went on to reassure Cindy. "She's home safe and sound and acting like she did nothing but laze around in her stall at Belmont. The race doesn't seem to have taken anything out of her. Why don't you go see her? I know she'd be glad to have you welcome her home."

"I will," Cindy said happily. She hurried down the aisle to Shining's stall door and peered in. Shining was resting in the back corner, a hoof cocked in relaxation. She perked up as soon as she saw Cindy and gave a whicker of greeting. Cindy went in and fed her a carrot and gave the filly a hug. It was great to see her looking so healthy after such a big race. "You were something the way you won that race," Cindy murmured. From down the aisle, she heard Ashleigh's voice.

"There was a real scene in the Townsend box after the race," she said.

"How did you find out—through the stable grapevine?" Len asked.

"No, actually Mike was right there," Ashleigh said.

"It wasn't pretty," Mike said. "Our seats were in the next section over from the Townsends'. After the race, Lavinia seemed shocked for a couple of minutes. Then she went into a tirade, cursing the jockey, cursing Ken Maddock. Clay Townsend told

Brad to get her back to the hotel and calm her down before she created even more of a scene."

Cindy heard the others tittering but didn't find the situation as funny as they did. To her, Lavinia was no laughing matter. If the woman was upset about Her Majesty, she was liable to take it out on everyone she could. Maybe Lavinia had forgotten about the watch during her stay at Belmont, but Cindy doubted Lavinia would forget once she got home. No doubt now she would remember her accusation with a vengeance. Only this time, if she called Cindy a thief, she would be right. All at once, Cindy wanted to see Glory. All day at school, she had thought of him guiltily, cooped up in the shed for hours, not knowing when she would come back.

The others had started to disperse. Cindy said goodbye to Shining and let herself out of the stall. Her foster father was coming down the aisle. "Oh, Cindy?" he said, stopping her. "I had an interesting phone call an hour ago from our neighbor—you know, the one you were asking about? Anyway, he was very friendly and polite, and he asked me if we'd seen one of the horses he was training loose on our property. The horse has been missing for a few days. He thinks he may have jumped the paddock fence. Do you know anything about it?"

Cindy felt the color drain from her face. So far, she

had not had to lie outright to her foster parents, but now she had no choice. "No, I don't," she replied.

"All right. I just wanted to make sure," Ian said. He turned and headed toward the office.

Cindy stared after him, dazed and desperately afraid that he had read the guilty expression on her face. If they knew she was hiding Glory, what would they do? She already had Lavinia's false accusations hanging over hear head. Would they wash their hands of her and send her away?

Over the next two days, Cindy continued to sneak food out to Glory, riding out on Bo or another exercise horse in the afternoons. Everyone was used to seeing her go on rides around the property, and no one said anything about the overstuffed saddle bags that went with her now. If anybody asked, Cindy was going to say that she was practicing for a long distance ride she wanted to take. She wanted to stay as close to the truth as possible, and, grim as it seemed, there was a chance of a very long distance ride in her and Glory's future. Running away still seemed impossible, but Cindy knew that if her secret were discovered, her fragile world could break apart in an instant. Once Lavinia had something else to threaten her with, her case seemed as good as lost.

Luckily, Samantha was busy every afternoon that week, helping Tor with the disabled riders they coached together. The group had been learning to ride as a drill team and was going to put on an exhibition to benefit the local hospital, so they had to practice every day. Before, Cindy had often volunteered to help Samantha out with the practices. She had fast become friends with Mandy, the youngest of the disabled riders, and she had made a point of encouraging the little girl to work hard at her riding. Cindy felt close to Mandy because she, too, knew what it was like to be on the outside of a world you wanted to belong to, looking in. That world, for both of them, was the world that Samantha and Ashleigh dwelled in. Mandy was fighting for the use of her legs, working hard on her riding; Cindy was fighting to find a permanent home where she was loved. In spite of many setbacks, neither of them was willing to give up. Whenever Cindy saw the little girl struggling to jump a fence, she reminded herself that she wasn't the only one with troubles. If Mandy would keep trying, she would, too. It seemed strange that right now, her own struggle kept Cindy from encouraging Mandy in hers, since she had to avoid Samantha as much as possible.

As for the morning feedings, Cindy simply left

124

about fifteen minutes early for the bus, then doubled back across the pastures. The McLeans had never been over-protective foster parents, and they tended to let Cindy do what she wanted with her time as long as her homework was done. Their trust was one of the things Cindy valued most about them. She felt lower than ever taking advantage of it. Seeing Glory safe in the shed was the only thing that kept her going.

But the shed had its problems, too. Cindy's main concern was how stifling it was for the energetic young horse. She could barely manage to get him out for a half hour's walk each day. She tried to jog him but couldn't keep up on foot with his big, ground-eating trot. Heather suggested ponying him off of Bo Jangles. That arrangement worked much better. Glory trotted along happily beside the old exercise horse. Unfortunately, they could only go a couple of hundred yards before coming to the woods and having to turn around.

Cindy ached when she had to return Glory to the shed. After less than half a week, he was practically climbing the walls. She knew she couldn't leave him there forever—maybe not even two weeks—and the thought that he was suffering made her unable to concentrate on anything else. Of course it wasn't as if he was being abused like before, but it was cruel nonetheless. Worrying, Cindy bit her nails down to the quick.

At school, she stared out the window, wracking her brains over and over for a better solution. For the first time since she had started at Henry Clay, she failed a test when the history teacher sprang a pop quiz on the class. Cindy had done the reading the night before, but she had been so distracted that nothing had sunk in. She looked over the questions in a panic, guessing on every one. It felt awful to be so unprepared; one of the things she had prided herself on was doing well at whatever school she was enrolled in. It made it easier when she was moved because she always got placed in the good classes with the smart kids. Her eyes swimming, Cindy got her quiz back and jammed it ashamedly into her pocket.

As she walked to the bus that afternoon, Heather came running up. She handed Cindy a manila envelope.

"What's this?" Cindy inquired, puzzled.

"Something from art class. Open it on the way home," Heather told her, dashing off to catch her own bus.

As soon as she had found a seat, Cindy opened the envelope and drew out its contents. It was a beautiful charcoal sketch of Glory, standing in front of the Whitebrook stables, his head raised proudly. On the back, Heather had written, "I wish I could do more to help."

Cindy felt tears spring to her eyes. If she could bring Glory to the Whitebrook stables, at least some of her troubles would be over.

On the Wednesday of that week, Cindy was returning on Bo Jangles from visiting the shed when she noticed a familiar car parked in front of the house. Her first thought was to flee: the dark blue sedan belonged to the Child Protection Services—to the people who had come before, the ones who had wanted to take her away. Their returning could only mean bad news. As slowly as she could, Cindy walked Bo Jangles back to the barn. She untacked him and groomed him extra-thouroghly, lingering over the job. Then she wiped off her tack. But it was no use. The intercom buzzed. Len answered it, but Cindy could hear Beth's voice asking anxiously if Cindy was around.

"Sure, she's right here," Len said.

"Please ask her to come up to the house. Some people are here who need to talk with her," Beth said. Cindy could tell that she was trying to sound casual.

"I'm going, Len," Cindy said, feeling defeated.

The scene in the house was even worse than she

had expected. Before going into the living room, Cindy listened at the door. One of the women was grilling the McLeans on Cindy's daily whereabouts. Cindy recognized Mrs. Lovell's voice.

"In the morning and afternoon she helps with the barn chores, goes riding—you know, she does what kids do," Ian McLean said wearily.

"What *some children* do, Mr. McLean," said Mrs. Lovell disapprovingly.

"So you're saying that she's completely unsupervised during the hours in which she is not in school?" the other woman demanded.

"No, she's not unsupervised—Len and Vic are around and I'm—" Mr. McLean began.

"Who are Len and Vic?" Mrs. Lovell interrupted.

There was a pause. Then Mr. McLean answered quietly, "Len is our stable manager and Vic is our head groom."

"Mr. and Mrs. McLean, it's really not surprising that she's gotten into trouble again," the other social worker said.

"What do you mean, 'gotten into trouble'?" Beth asked. "She's been a model kid. She's friendly, polite, eager to pitch in, and totally honest." Cindy winced at Beth's description.

"That's not the information we've been given," Mrs. Lovell said. "We received calls from a very prominent Lexington family and the police regarding the theft of a valuable gold watch. According to the complaint, Cynthia was visiting the stables at Townsend Acres where she was allowed to wander off by herself. She then stole—"

"Enough!" Ian thundered. "The Townsends have no evidence whatsoever that Cindy took Lavinia's watch. Cindy's just a convenient scapegoat for Lavinia because Cindy happens to be an orphan. You have no right to accuse her!"

"I've asked Cindy to come in," Beth said. "I'm sure when you see her and talk to her, you'll really be delighted with her progress."

Seizing the opportunity to make an entrance, Cindy swung open the door. Her stomach was knotted in fear, but she greeted her foster parents and shook hands with the two welfare workers.

"How are you, Cindy?" Mrs. Lovell asked.

"I'm good—I'm fine. I love it here," Cindy replied in a nervous rush.

"You look tired. You've got circles under your eyes," the woman commented.

"Really?" Cindy asked. She couldn't think of anything else to say. She couldn't exactly explain that she looked tired because she was hiding a runaway horse and losing sleep over that and Lavinia's accusation.

"We understand you spent the month of August at the Saratoga Racetrack?" Mrs. Lovell said. Her lips turned down with distaste at the word "racetrack."

"Yes" Cindy answered. *How had they found that out,* she wondered.

"And what did you do there?"

"Helped with horses, mucked stables, groomed, cleaned tack," Cindy said.

Mrs. Lovell shot a look to the McLeans, then looked back to Cindy. "It sounds as though you were worked pretty hard."

"Oh, no," Cindy replied. "I wanted to help. I didn't have to. I love the horses and I love taking care of them."

"Still, I can't think of a racetrack as the ideal environment for a young girl. There are bound to be unsavory influences."

"Wait a minute," Ian McLean interrupted. "I think you have some misconceptions about racetrack life."

Mrs. Lovell ignored him and spoke to Cindy. "Do you get up early?"

Cindy let out a deep breath. Finally there was a question she knew how to answer. "Yes, I get up at around five every day," she said proudly. She glanced at the McLeans for approval, but they only frowned worriedly.

"My, five o'clock," the woman repeated. "It's no wonder you have circles under your eyes."

"But I go to bed before—" Cindy tried to say, but the woman cut her off.

"Tell me, do you find that the schedule here interferes with your schoolwork?"

"No, ma'am. Not at all," Cindy answered. She knew she sounded defensive, but she couldn't help it.

"So you've been doing well in school?" the woman prompted her.

Cindy shifted uneasily in her seat. Did she have to tell about the one bad grade she had received? "Yes, I've been doing well," she said.

"I understand from your history teacher that you failed a quiz yesterday," the woman said.

"That's not fair!" Cindy burst out. "That's the first time I've ever done badly all fall!"

"All right, all right. But remember: it's better to be honest, dear, and tell the *whole* truth," the woman said.

"Fine. I failed a pop quiz," Cindy said sullenly.

"That's better." The questioning went on for nearly half-an-hour. Cindy tried to be polite, but she felt herself growing angrier and angrier as the woman twisted her words around until she hardly knew what she was saying. It was as if they wanted her to say that she was neglected and miserable and a thief.

131

As soon as she was excused, she left the room, pausing on the other side of the door.

"An entire month living at a racetrack? Why weren't we informed? I suppose you think being surrounded by gamblers and drug addicts all day is suitable for a child?" Mrs. Lovell exclaimed.

"What gamblers? My wife and I never bet," Mr. McLean protested. "And as I tried to say earlier, you have some misconceptions of track life. Yes, there are occasional problems with drugs, but there are benevolent organizations actively working to keep drugs off the backside. And we certainly didn't expose Cindy to any of the rougher elements."

"How can you be sure? I doubt you were constantly at Cindy's side," Mrs. Lovell retorted. "I think we may as well call a halt to this meeting. I'll be filing a report with the Kentucky authorities. From what I've observed, this is not a satisfactory environment for Cynthia. We have to consider all aspects of her life here. The girl has a history of maladjustment and misbehavior. You're both busy with your jobs all day, you leave her to hang out at racetracks by herself—it's no wonder she would resort to stealing."

Cindy fled the hallway before she could hear anymore. She ran upstairs and threw herself on her bed, sobbing. All Mrs. Lovell had wanted to hear about were the problems. They hadn't even given her a chance to say how much she loved Whitebrook or how happy her days had been. It was true that the McLeans were busy people. But they always had time for her. And they were busy in the best kind of way—doing what they loved. They loved their jobs, they loved animals, and they loved each other.

"Nobody at Whitebrook could ever be lonely," Cindy sobbed into her pillow. She had so many friends there, she could hardly count them. There were Sammy and Tor, Ashleigh and Mike, Mr. Reese, Len and the grooms—and they all liked her and watched out for her and encouraged her. Why couldn't the social workers look beyond their prejudices and realize that?

That night, Cindy tossed and turned in bed. The afternoon's events had devastated her, but, even more than the unfairness of the welfare women, the knowledge that she was lying to the McLeans kept her awake. What was the use of protesting her innocence about the watch when she was guilty of a worse crime than the one she had been accused of? After staring at the ceiling for almost an hour, Cindy rose from her bed. She slipped a bathrobe on over her pajamas and walked down the hall. Samantha was out on a date with Tor, and her room was empty. Ian and Beth were sound asleep in their room. The house felt strange to Cindy, as if she didn't belong in it anymore. She tried to read in the living room, but the page swam before her eyes. Her conscience wouldn't let her sit still. The words "liar! thief!" kept running through her mind.

Without thinking about what she was doing, Cindy slipped on a pair of boots and went outside. A nearly full moon shone brightly in the night sky, illuminating the white paddock fences. Cindy walked quickly along the edge of the pastures. Soon she could make out the dark outline of the shed. "It's only me, boy," she said as she slipped inside. The colt nickered softly. "I just had to come see you, Glory. Everything's terrible. They're going to make me leave here. I know they are! And then what'll I do with you? The McLeans will hate me when they find out I lied to them!"

Bursting into tears, Cindy flung her arms around the gray's neck. "Maybe we'll run away," she sobbed. "Somewhere where you'll be safe from those men, and I'll be safe from the welfare workers, once and for all." But where was that place? Cindy wondered.

All of a sudden, a white shape pounced from Glory's back, landing on Cindy's shoulders. In spite of herself, Cindy laughed through her tears. "Oh, Imp, you can come, too," she told the kitten. She carefully detached him from her body and set him down.

It was a beautiful night, and Cindy figured she might as well take Glory out for a walk even though it was late. There was no point in trying to sleep when she was so upset. She clipped a lead line to the horse's halter and led him out. Imp scampered along behind, slinking through the grass and hunting imaginary prey. Glory walked contentedly by Cindy's side. Every so often he paused to nibble at something on the ground or to listen to a distant sound. "It's okay. We're safe together here," Cindy said, to reassure herself more than Glory. Every time she looked at the woods, she got scared—she imagined the two men coming out with their whips, chasing her down and taking Glory away—but the horse seemed calm. Cindy had never seen him look so beautiful. The moonlight turned his gray coat silver, and he shone like a phantom horse in the night.

Watching him move, Cindy was seized by the desire to try riding him—just to sit on his back for a few minutes while they meandered down the trail. She led Glory over to the pasture fence, climbed it, and swung gently onto the broad back. For a split second, Cindy was afraid that being ridden would remind him of being abused, but Glory stood calmly. He just ambled a few steps forward and then stopped to graze. To Cindy, sitting on the beautiful horse was a dream come true. Her heart swelled to think that he trusted her enough to allow her to. His back was much higher off the ground than Bo Jangles', and when he walked, he felt like a coiled spring of energy. Cindy forgot that she was wearing pajamas and a bathrobe and imagined herself in Whitebrook racing silks, flying down the home stretch.

"I wish you could meet Shining," Cindy told Glory. "I'm sure you'd get along really well. She's beautiful, too, in a different way. And Sammy's great. She rides race horses every day."

Thinking about Samantha made Cindy realize that she ought to get back to the house. She felt better just having come out here, and she didn't want the McLeans to wake up and find her missing. After all, she told herself sternly, nothing had been decided yet about her future, grim as it might seem.

"I'm going to come out every night and ride you, Glory. How does that sound?" Cindy asked. She gently nudged the horse back toward the shed.

Without any warning, Glory tensed underneath her, pricking his ears nervously. "What is it, boy? What's wrong?" Cindy rubbed his neck to try to soothe him. She followed his gaze toward the edge of the woods. What she saw paralyzed her with fear. Just like in her worst nightmare, two shadowy figures were approaching them. Never before had Cindy known such pure terror. With white knuckles, she clutched Glory's mane, feeling the horse tremble beneath her. The figures came closer and closer. A scream rose in Cindy's throat, but she couldn't seem to find her voice. Desperately, she tried to turn Glory. The horse spun around and bolted, Cindy clinging wildly to his neck. Too late she saw the white pasture fence gleaming in front of her. In blind fear, Glory galloped straight for it. At the last second, he swerved violently, catapulting Cindy over his head. Cindy felt a strange weightlessness as she was thrown through the air, then the sickening crunch of her body slamming into the earth.

11

"CINDY, DON'T MOVE. DON'T TRY TO GET UP. YOU'VE HAD the wind knocked out of you, but you're going to be okay. That's right. Just lie still and take deep breaths."

Cindy stared numbly at the ground, listening to the familiar voice tell her what to do. She could dimly make out two pairs of feet in front of her. She drew a long breath and let it out slowly. Then she felt a pair of hands helping her to a sitting position. "Careful, now, careful," the voice said. No, it couldn't be, but it was—Samantha's voice! But that meant—

"How do you feel, Cindy?" Samantha asked.

Cindy looked up in a daze. "Sammy?" she croaked.

"That's right, Cin—you took quite a spill," Samantha said.

At that, Cindy began to babble uncontrollably. "I

fell off Glory! I let him down! The two awful men came out of the woods, and I didn't know what to do. They must have gotten him and taken him away—I knew this would happen! Oh, Sammy I tried so hard to save him, but it didn't matter. I'll never see him again!"

"Cindy, Cindy—shhh, it's okay," Samantha said. She put her arms on Cindy's shoulders to quiet her. Then she pointed. "Is that, by any chance, Glory?"

Cindy stared. A few yards away, Tor was standing holding the big gray horse. He grinned when Cindy nodded incredulously. "That's him," she said in utter shock.

Samantha smiled. "Then Tor and I are your two 'awful men'," she said. "We came home from our date and, since it was such a nice night, we decided to take a stroll around the pastures. Then we saw someone on horseback and came to check things out. We realized it was you, but the horse halted before we could call out to you. So, where did this horse come from, anyway? He's sure not one of ours."

"Oh, Sammy, I'm so sorry," Cindy cried. "I panicked. I thought it was Glory's owners—the neighbors— coming to take him away."

"Ah, I thought I recognized him. He's even more beautiful up close," Samantha said. "Now suppose you start at the beginning and tell me why he's here

139

and how you came to be riding him at one o'clock in the morning."

Cindy paused for a minute. Suddenly she knew what she had to do. "Sammy, I want to start from the beginning, but I can't tell just you. I have to tell your parents, too. I've been keeping this secret from them, hiding Glory in the shed. I've lied, and I stole—not a watch, a horse."

Samantha gave Cindy a hug. "Let's head back and hear your story," she said. The two of them joined Tor and put Glory back in the shed.

"Wow, you're really handy," Tor exclaimed when he saw the makeshift stable.

"I'll say. This place is cozy," Samantha agreed, "but I think he'll be happier in a stall in one of our stables."

Cindy tried to smile. She only hoped Beth and Ian would be as enthusiastic about the transformation of the shed into a secret hiding place.

"I wish we didn't have to leave him here," Cindy said.

"I know," Samantha said, "but it might just be better to go back alone and talk to Beth and Dad first instead of surprising them with a brand new horse. Besides, a few more hours out here isn't going to hurt him."

"Then you think there's a chance they might say to bring him back to the stables?" Cindy asked.

140

"You know Dad—no matter how annoyed he gets at an owner, he always puts the horse's well-being first," Samantha reminded her.

Deep inside, Cindy felt a spark of hope.

Back at the cottage, all of the lights were ablaze. Cindy paused nervously at the front door. Samantha nudged her and mouthed "good luck." Tor gave her a thumbs-up sign. Crossing her fingers, Cindy followed them into the kitchen.

"Samantha, Tor, do you have any idea where— Cindy, you're all right!" Beth exclaimed. She hung up the phone she was holding and embraced Cindy. "Ian and I just woke up and saw that you were gone. I was about to call the police. I thought you'd run away!"

"No, I didn't run away. I did think about it, though," Cindy admitted sheepishly.

"I'd like to strangle those social workers," Mr. McLean said angrily. "They had no right to question you the way they did."

"They're not the reason I was going to run away," Cindy said. She stared uncomfortably at her feet. *Anyway, they were right,* she thought. *Only it's not that Whitebrook is wrong for me—it's that I'm wrong for it. I don't deserve to live here, with such good, honest people.*

Tor cleared his throat loudly, looking at Samantha. "Listen, uh, maybe I ought to be going," he suggested.

"No, Tor, you don't have to go. I want everyone to hear," Cindy said.

"What is it, honey? You look so troubled," Beth said gently.

Cindy took a deep breath. Then she looked up at her foster parents. "I didn't steal Lavinia's watch, but I am guilty—of taking a horse that belongs to someone else." Slowly at first, then in a torrent of explanation, Cindy recounted the past few weeks. She told about her visits to the neighbors' field, about finding Glory loose, about hiding him in the shed, and, finally, about what had happened that night.

"Those men treated him so badly that he ran away. I know that's what happened because I've done the same thing. I just couldn't give him back to them," Cindy finished. There. She had told them everything. Now it was up to them to decide her fate. The McLeans had listened quietly while she spoke. "Well, Cindy," her foster father said finally, "That horse does belong to someone else. He's not yours to take."

"I know," Cindy sobbed. "But he's so beautiful, and they were so cruel to him!"

"I understand how you feel, but there's a right and a wrong way to go about things. This is the same horse we've talked about?" he asked.

142

"Yes. I wanted you to see how he was being abused, but when he got loose, I just didn't know what to do, so I took him, and I didn't say anything to you."

"And I forgot to ask you how he was doing," Mr. McLean said, his voice thoughtful. "He's in the shed now?"

Cindy nodded.

"Wait till you see how she fixed it up for him," Tor put in. "It's great!" Cindy shot him a grateful look.

Mr. McLean glanced at the clock on the kitchen wall. "Well, I see it's almost two o'clock in the morning," he said, "but I doubt anyone's very sleepy now. Let's go have a look at him."

"Like this?" Beth asked, glancing down at her nightgown and slippers.

"Why not? It doesn't seem to have stopped Cindy," Ian pointed out.

"All right then," Beth agreed.

Cindy felt freer than she had in weeks, as though a huge weight had been lifted from her shoulders. Her foster father's stern words rang in her mind, but somehow he didn't look fierce as he trooped out to the shed in his pajamas. Samantha and Tor linked arms with her companionably, and the three of them led the way.

When they got to the shed, Glory gave Cindy

his usual whinny of greeting. He nuzzled her happily, looking for carrots. But when he saw the others, he started nervously. Cindy soothed him as much as she could. "They're your friends, too, Glory," she whispered. She hoped that that would prove to be the case and that her foster parents wouldn't send the horse back to his owner.

Mr. McLean went into the stall quietly, speaking soothingly as he inspected the horse. He ran a hand down each of his legs, looked in his mouth, and then stepped back to study him.

"You two are right about one thing," he said to Cindy and Samantha. "This is one beauty of a horse. He's a Thoroughbred and probably a two-year-old. He's a valuable animal."

Cindy was thrilled to hear her suspicions confirmed. She just hoped Glory's good breeding would make her foster father want to keep him on the farm. She stroked the gray neck, half-listening as her Mr. McLean mused aloud.

"It's funny, but I didn't think that the neighbors could afford an animal like this with the kind of operation they're running. When I talked to the man, he gave me the impression that he was only doing local stuff, not big racing. But Cindy," he added, suddenly stern again, "You do realize that you shouldn't have hidden him, don't you? You should have told us right away. The fact that he's been gone half a week certainly doesn't help your cause. Especially considering all the trouble we've had with Lavinia Townsend."

Cindy looked down. "Yes, I know," she said. She bit her lip hard to keep from crying.

"Dad," Samantha said, "don't be too hard on Cindy. Given the situation, I would have done the same thing she did."

Mr. McLean's face softened as he looked at the two girls' earnest faces. "All right, just so that it's clear," he said. "Now, let's take this horse back and give him a real stall for the rest of the night. We'll examine him more carefully tomorrow. I, for one, have to get up in four hours," he added.

"You're not going to call the neighbors?" Cindy asked.

"Not until I do a little more investigating."

Cindy could hardly believe her ears. Glory was actually coming back with her to the Whitebrook stables, just as she had dreamed one day he would. She didn't know whom to hug first—her foster parents, Samantha, Tor, Glory—or the feline creature that was attacking her leg. "Imp!" Cindy cried, scooping up the white fur ball.

"Who's this?" Beth asked curiously.

"Are you guilty of cat-napping, too, Miss Blake?" Tor teased.

Cindy smiled. "I guess I haven't told you *everything*," she said.

The next day, Cindy could barely keep her eyes open at school. She could imagine what Mrs. Lovell would say if she could see how tired she looked now! But she also felt a huge sense of relief about having told the McLeans the truth. She had checked on Glory before school, delighted to find that he looked happy in his temporary home. Len had promised to turn him out for a few hours to let him stretch his legs.

Neither Cindy nor Heather touched one bite of their lunch that day. Cindy was too busy pouring out the story of the night before, and Heather was too excited to eat. When the bell rang for the next period, Heather impulsively gave Cindy a hug. "I'm so happy for you!" she cried.

On the bus home, Cindy realized that having someone to share her happiness with made her all the more lucky. She didn't know what was going to happen to Glory or to herself any more than she had before. But for the moment, at least, she was happy.

When Cindy entered the training barn that afternoon, she was surprised to find Glory cross-tied in the aisle, surrounded by Ashleigh, Mike, Len, and Ian.

"So here's the horse thief," Ashleigh said teasingly.

"You've been busier than all of the rest of us put together, Cindy."

For an instant, Cindy's face paled. Then Ashleigh grinned at her reassuringly. "I would have done the same thing," Ashleigh said.

"And you may have stumbled onto something," Mike added mysteriously.

"Is Glory all right?" Cindy asked. She noticed that he seemed ill at ease with so many people around. She laid a comforting hand on his neck.

"He's fine, thanks to your treating this nasty welt on his flank," her foster father said, frowning. He pointed to the scar where the welt had healed.

"That's plain ugly, and all day he's seemed really nervous around us," Ashleigh said.

Mike spoke up. "As we all know from Cindy, this is an abused horse. If we wanted more proof, we've got it: he's scared of people, and he's scared of whips. But the question is, why would anyone mistreat a horse like this? A valuable, registered Thoroughbred."

"He's registered?" Cindy asked.

Mike nodded. He moved quietly to Glory's head. After stroking the gray nose for a few minutes, he pulled up the horse's upper lip to show Cindy the tatooed number inside. All registered Thouroughbreds were tatooed and blood typed. "I'm going to get in touch with the authorities," Mike decided.

Mr. McLean nodded. "Good idea."

Cindy's heart leapt for joy at hearing this exchange. In the back of her mind, she knew that the longer it took to find out about Glory's situation, the longer he could stay. While Mike went to make the call, she seized the opportunity to give the gray a thorough grooming. Ashleigh stayed to help out. Together they fussed over Glory, making up stories about his past. At the end of the grooming session, Cindy was thrilled to hear Ashleigh whisper, "I know I shouldn't say this, but I'm half hoping he'll have to stay at Whitebrook indefinitely."

Mr. McLean walked up frowning. "Now this is strange. It seems the authorities don't know anything about a missing horse." He paused for a moment, speculating. "Funny that the guy calls me about it but doesn't report it to the people who might be able to help get the horse back."

"Funny indeed," Ashleigh replied. "It sounds downright suspicious. It doesn't make sense unless he's up to something shifty. So what are you going to do now?"

Cindy listened intently. She had been wondering the same thing but had been too afraid to ask.

"Mike is going to put a call in to the Jockey Club tomorrow to see if he can find out anything about the horse through his registration number. I have to say,"

Ian added, turning to Cindy, "that I'm sorry I didn't pursue the matter further on my own once you told me what was going on. Your suspicions were obviously right."

Cindy gulped, unable to speak. No adult had ever apologized to her before, and she had no idea of how to react. She felt herself turning beet red with embarrassment. After all, she had purposefully dropped the subject with her foster father once she had hidden Glory in the shed.

Mr. McLean thoughtfully studied the colt and shook his head. "Mike is right: I can't believe anyone would abuse a horse like this."

After everyone drifted off, Cindy put Glory back in his stall. He had been given a large box stall a few doors down from Shining. Cindy spent a long time standing with him, feeding him treats and talking. Concentrating on Glory's circumstances helped her to forget about her own predicament. For the moment, they were both safe at Whitebrook. But one phone call—from the neighbor, from the Jockey Club, from the Child Protection Services—could change everything.

Even more worrisome than a phone call was the thought of the neighbors showing up and finding their horse. If they discovered him, Cindy didn't see what Mike or her foster father could do or say to make a difference. The older man would be sure to recognize Cindy from the time he had caught her trespassing and he would certainly want to press charges. What kind of a foster home would there be for a minor convicted of stealing? Probably no home at all—just a juvenile correction center. Cindy shuddered.

Before she left the stall, she looked solemnly into Glory's trusting brown eyes. She twined her fingers through his dark gray mane. "I'll be with you, no matter what, boy," she vowed. Even, Cindy thought grimly, if it meant leaving Whitebrook.

12

HEATHER PRACTICALLY POUNCED ON CINDY AT LUNCH the next day. "Tell me what happened! Is Glory still at Whitebrook?"

Cindy was eager to update her friend. "He is for now, so keep your fingers crossed," she said. "Actually, the whole thing is turning into a mystery. We're waiting to hear from the Jockey Club about Glory's identification. The neighbors are up to something fishy. They didn't report his absence to the police even though they called Ian about it," she said.

"*Huh?*" Heather said.

Cindy laughed. "It's funny: I thought that everything would be over if I told the McLeans about Glory. I figured he'd be sent back to the neighbors, and I'd be packed off to another foster home right

151

away for stealing him. Instead, things have gotten really complicated, and I have no idea what's going to happen to either of us." As clearly as she could, Cindy explained the current situation.

"So when the Jockey Club calls, you'll know who Glory really is?" Heather asked when Cindy had finished.

"We hope so," Cindy said. "And once they find out his true identity, we'll be able to find out if he's been stolen and actually belongs to someone else."

"Then what will happen?" Heather asked.

"I don't know," Cindy said. "But for now at least, Glory is at home with me."

"That's funny," Heather said after a pause.

"What's funny?" Cindy asked.

"It's just that I've never heard you refer to Whitebrook as 'home' before," Heather replied.

Cindy looked at her friend, startled. "I guess with Glory there, it makes it feel like home," she said lightly, brushing off Heather's observation.

But on the ride home, Heather's comment kept coming back to Cindy. It was obvious what the slip meant: even though her own future at Whitebrook was in jeopardy, Cindy had come to think of the farm as her true home. Now she had let down all of her defenses—just when she should have been preparing for the worst. Now she knew she could imagine no other home than Whitebrook.

When she got off the bus, Cindy went straight to Mike's office. He was just hanging up the phone. Ashleigh and her foster father were sitting on the couch.

"Cindy, glad you're here," Mike said. "Your mystery has taken an interesting turn. The tattoo on—Glory, is that what you call him?—corresponds to a two-year-old Thoroughbred named Parkway Runner who has never been raced. We've been trying to get in touch with the owners—who, by the way, live in Maryland, not next door—but we haven't had any luck so far. Anyway, the Jockey Club wanted us to get our horse's blood type and see if that corresponds, too. The vet came this morning, and he's mailed off the sample to the lab. So all we can do now is wait. We are going to hold onto this colt until we've finished checking out all possible angles."

Then Mr. McLean spoke up. "Cindy, the truth is, we think your Glory was stolen and that these men are trying to pull a switch."

"A switch?" Cindy repeated.

Her foster father nodded. "Unfortunately, it's a classic racetrack crime. They take a horse with talent and change its ID number to match that of a horse who is a dud. Of course, the two horses have to have similar coloring and physical characteristics. Then they run the proven horse in a race under the other horse's identity. The bettors don't back the horse, thinking its an unproven maiden. The horse wins, as these crooks knew it would, and they win a bundle on the bets they've placed. My guess is that the real Parkway Runner may be dead. Probably Glory's original tattoo number only needed a few changes to make it match Parkway Runner's."

Ian paused with an angry frown. "Then they repeat the cycle all over. When the horse that's winning starts getting short odds, they pull him out of training, saying he's had an injury. Remember, since these crooks stay away from the big races for fear of getting caught, they win more money on bets than they do in purses. When the winning horse supposedly returns to racing, it's not him, but another substitute, who this time will be a loser. The horse is bet up as a favorite because of his supposed past record. The crooks bet on other horses in the field who look like they have a chance of winning against the dud they've substituted. Their substitute horse crosses the wire near the end of the field. One of the horses the crooks have bet on wins at fairly long odds, and again, they win big bucks. Of course, they don't keep racing at the same tracks. They move from track to track all over the country, staying in the low allowance ranks. Otherwise, someone might start putting two and two together."

"Poor Glory!" Cindy cried at the end of the explanation.

Ashleigh nodded. "Poor Glory is right: now you know why those men's methods of training may have been a bit coarse, to say the least."

Cindy nodded glumly. She felt like she should have been more eager to know the mystery behind Glory's past, but instead, all she felt was sympathy for the trauma he must have gone through if her foster father's explanation was right. And she was more frightened than ever that the men would discover that they were keeping Glory. "What if they show up here and ask for him back?" she asked, her voice barely a whisper.

Her foster father put a reassuring hand on her shoulder. "They can't know the horse is here. Fortunately, you kept him hidden before, and now he's out of sight. The only people we've told are the authorities. They're as interested as we are in getting to the bottom of this."

"How long will it take for the blood sample to be processed?" Cindy inquired.

"We should hear in about two days," Mike answered.

Cindy nodded. *Then we have at least two more days together*, she thought.

For Cindy, the next two days were a combination of bliss and fear. She was incredibly happy knowing that Glory was "hers" for forty-eight hours and she forced herself not to think about what would happen afterward. "I'm going to take advantage of the time we have together," she told Heather in school after inviting her to come over and see him that afternoon.

Heather was delighted by the sight of Glory in a Whitebrook stall. "He looks like he belongs there, Cindy!" she cried.

Cindy nodded, grinning. "Just like in your sketch. Let's pretend he's living here for good," she said.

Heather agreed readily. They spent the rest of the afternoon with the horse, brushing him, walking him—staying close to the barns, so he wouldn't be seen—and playing with him as if her were a pet. Glory loved all of the attention.

"If that horse looked any happier, he'd be smiling," Len remarked when he passed the girls on his afternoon rounds.

"Oh, Len, isn't he beautiful?" Cindy asked.

The old groom paused, casting an appraising eye over the well-proportioned colt. "Well, I'm not one to go around calling horses 'beautiful' and naming them 'Glory' and 'Shining,' but I do have to admit that that is one fine looking animal. Looks like he could be fast, too."

Cindy glowed with pride.

As predicted, two days after Mike had sent off the sample to the lab, the results came in. Mike immediately phoned the Jockey Club with the information and received a call back that afternoon. The blood type did not match that of the horse registered as Parkway Runner. "It's going to take a while to trace our horse since they don't know his real—original—tattoo number. They're going to have to trace through all the registered two- and three-year-old grays with matching blood types and then contact the owners to see if they've reported a stolen horse," he announced to the expectant group.

"And so—" Cindy began.

Mike smiled. "And so, Glory can stay at Whitebrook if we'll have him. And my father, Ash, and I want him to stay."

The group burst into spontaneous applause. Glory was becoming popular with everyone. Although he had been head-shy and timid around people, especially men, at first, he was responding well to gentle handling.

On his way out of the office, Vic Taleski stopped to

speak with Cindy. "Good job, Cindy. We're all very proud of you," he said.

Cindy stared after him, baffled. "But I didn't have anything to do with—" she started to say, but the groom was out the door.

The following week Cindy was busier than ever. Every afternoon, she raced from the bus to the barn, changing in the tack room to have a few extra minutes with the horses. With all of the excitement concerning Glory, Cindy had almost forgotten that Samantha had entered Shining in the Queen Elizabeth II Challenge Cup at Keeneland near the end of October. Samantha had enlisted Cindy's help in getting the filly ready. Cindy suspected that the older girl just wanted to keep her thoughts occupied. Either way, Cindy was eager to help. She loved working with the filly, and now that Glory's future was on hold, she did have plenty of time to let her mind wander to her own future. She still could not hear the telephone ring without jumping, sure that any day the social workers would call. She knew that it was just a matter of time before the state responded to their report.

Grooming Glory took whatever time was left after working on Shining. Around others, the horse was more relaxed than he had been but still on guard, wary of anyone that approached him too quickly. At mealtimes, he bolted his grain, pacing back and forth. But with Cindy, he was docile as an old pony, rubbing his head against her, dozing off while she fussed over his mane or painted polish on his hooves. The peaceful times she spent with Glory were the times Cindy felt the happiest. Sometimes she took him out for a little stroll, close to the barn, where they wouldn't be seen by passersby. She would look out over Whitebrook, memorizing every perfect detail about the place. She imagined being the first to really ride Glory—under saddle, on a track, where she was sure he belonged.

But sometimes dark thoughts broke through her daydreams. Far from dropping her charges, Lavinia was trying harder than ever to pin the missing watch on Cindy. Cindy overheard snatches of conversation between her foster parents late at night when they sat up talking in the kitchen, and she noticed the way all of the McLeans looked at her—they smiled, but their smiles seemed sad. Mrs. Lovell had returned once to question Cindy further about the incident. Cindy had remained calm during the session, but afterwards she had run out to the stable and buried her face in Glory's mane, weeping profusely.

"Why do they keep coming back?" she cried. "What

else can I tell them? I didn't take her watch! At least you believe me, Glory." It still seemed impossible to Cindy that she might be punished for something she hadn't done. At her old foster homes, it wouldn't have surprised her. But Whitebrook was different. Everyone had been kind to her from the first. She had believed, against all odds, that somehow she would be safe here. But then, she hadn't known Lavinia Townsend.

The morning after the second visit from Mrs. Lowell, a Saturday, Cindy woke up feeling uneasy. She ran out to the barn to check on Glory. He was munching hay contentedly, and Len said that, as far as he knew, the Jockey Club hadn't turned up any new information yet. Still, Cindy couldn't shake the worried premonition that something terrible was going to happen. She hardly touched her breakfast and helped Beth with the dishes in a daze.

"What's wrong, Cindy? You seem like you're in another world," Beth said gently.

Cindy looked up at her foster mother with troubled eyes. She licked her dry lips nervously. "Beth, I don't know why, but I feel like something bad is going to happen," she said. There was no point in keeping her worry to herself anymore now that everything was out of her control.

Beth gave Cindy a sharp look. "Come sit down a minute, Cindy," she said.

Cindy placed the glass she was drying on the dish rack. The room felt like it was spinning. Why did Beth look so guilty and sad all of a sudden? Cindy sat down on the couch numbly, her heart pounding in her chest.

Beth took both of Cindy's hands in her own. "Honey, I wasn't going to say anything to you yet, but you seem to have sensed that something is wrong . . . " Beth let her voice trail off, her eyes searching Cindy's face. Finally, she resumed. "We got a call late last night. Mrs. Lovell is coming back this morning. She heard from the state. It's not looking good, Cindy. We—we tried to explain how happy you've been, but nothing we've told them seems to make a difference. They're prejudiced against Ian for being a horseman, and I guess they think I'm not much better. I'm sure the Townsends haven't helped, either. Lavinia wrote to the state authorities, and Brad is backing her up. But I promise you, even if today's news is bad, we're not going to give up this fight." Beth stopped, her voice cracking.

Cindy stared at the floor. She felt nothing. Not shock or dismay or outrage. She felt beyond any emotions at all. It was just like before—before the McLeans had become her foster parents. They—

whoever they were—had tried to take her away then, too.

"Cindy?" Beth prompted her gently.

"Yeah," she said listlessly, keeping her eyes on the floor.

"I—we don't know for sure—the report might be better than we think. . . ."

"It's okay, Beth. I know it's not your fault."

"Oh, honey! I'm so sorry! Ian and I have tried everything! We just don't know what to do anymore!" Beth stood up and ran to the sink, her face in her hands.

Cindy stared at her sympathetically. She could feel sorry for Beth. But for herself, bad news was nothing new. She had always known that Whitebrook was too good to be true. That was why she had never called it 'home.' It had been a mistake to relax here, thinking she might have a chance to stay. Everything would have been better if she had run away the minute Samantha had found her in the twin foals' stall. Now she would have to go through the pain of realizing she was an orphan all over again. She knew that the pain would come—maybe not right away, but after the initial shock had passed, she would be as sad as she had ever been. Before, she couldn't have imagined a place like Whitebrook or people like the McLeans or Ashleigh or Mike. Now she knew what happiness looked like—felt like. It was worse than never having known it.

Later that morning, the blue sedan pulled up in the driveway. Cindy stared out the bedroom window. Mrs. Lovell got out of the car, looked around at her surroundings, and shook her head distastefully. Cindy heard someone open the door, then her foster father called up to her to come down.

Cindy rose and looked at herself in the mirror. She looked different than when she had arrived at Whitebrook. Her face was fuller, and it was tanned from being outside all fall. Before, she had worn her blond hair any which way, mostly letting it hang in her face so that she could hide behind it. Now, she had had it trimmed at a Lexington salon and she kept it pulled back in a ponytail so that it stayed out of her face when she rode and worked around the horses. Her clothes—her jeans and flannel shirt—weren't more than a month or two old, and she had a bureau full of new things.

Cindy stared at her reflection for a couple of minutes more. Then she leaned close and whispered fiercely to herself, "You may look different now, but you're still the same orphan underneath." She turned away and went to meet Mrs. Lovell.

"We'll be waiting for you in the kitchen," Ian said gravely.

Cindy entered the room and stood just inside the door. "Hello, Cindy," the woman greeted her brightly.

"Hello," said Cindy.

Mrs. Lovell shuffled a stack of papers importantly. "Well, we might as well get right to the point. As I've told the McLeans, our board, working with the state, has decided that with the evidence we've gathered here, it's important for us to find a new home for you—one where you'll be happier and have a better family life."

"But I'm happy here!" Cindy cried. Dazed with horror, she grabbed the woman's arm desperately. "Don't you see? Don't you care that I love it here?" She began to wail hysterically.

Mrs. Lovell disentangled herself from Cindy's grip. "I know you *like* it here, Cindy, but children don't always know what's best for them. We're going to find a very nice new home for you just as soon as we can."

Unable to control herself, Cindy threw herself down on the sofa and began pounding the pillows. She didn't hear Mrs. Lovell leave the room or her foster father enter. A pair of strong arms wrapped around her and held her until she had calmed down and could breathe without choking on her tears.

"I'm so sorry," Mr. McLean said, repeating the

words again and again, and stroking her hair to comfort her.

That afternoon, Cindy went out to the training barn. She almost didn't want to go—seeing the horses would be hard to bear. But she knew that her time with them was almost over, and she couldn't stay away. Whether it was a few days or a couple of weeks before the social worker found her a new foster family hardly seemed to matter now that she knew she had no chance of staying. Nothing the McLeans could do would help now that the state had handed down its decision. She had cried so hard after Mrs. Lovell had gone that her face felt strange, her eyes puffy and tight from the tears.

Samantha was in the barn, grooming Shining on the cross-ties. Cindy offered to help. She picked up a soft cloth and began to rub the copper-flecked coat as she had so many times before. The two girls worked silently side by side. Finally Samantha said, "Cindy, Beth told me the news."

Cindy looked up at her foster sister. "It's all settled. They're going to take me away," she said dully.

Samantha put down the brush she was holding and put her hands on Cindy's shoulders. "No, Cindy.

Not if we can stop them. You'll be there to see Shining win again," she said, a determined edge to her voice.

Cindy made an attempt to smile but failed. She knew Samantha meant what she said. But she also knew the state authorities. "Sammy, don't feel bad for me. It's not your fault. If the State thinks I'm a thief, there's nothing you can do. No matter what your parents say, the Child Protection Services will believe Lavinia's story."

"But Cindy, you can't give up hope!" Samantha pleaded.

Cindy met the older girl's eyes. She knew, all at once, that for her sake and for all of the McLeans, she couldn't let herself slip into not hoping, even if it meant greater disappointment in the end. "I'll try not to," she promised.

Cindy spent the next few hours in Glory's stall, a frightened lump in her throat. She cuddled Imp close to her and leaned against the colt's broad, gray back. "Why does it have to be this way, Glory? Why do our lives have to be in other people's hands?" she whispered. It was ironic, really: just when Glory's life had started to look up, her own had become bleak. Still, nothing made her happier than watching the way the horse had responded to his new home. He no longer started nervously when men entered the barn, and his eyes had lost their tortured look.

Cindy wondered how long he would be able to stay at Whitebrook. If they didn't find his owner, and he stayed for more than a few weeks, Mr. McLean might start to train him. Ashleigh or Samantha would probably be the first to ride him under saddle. Thinking of one of them mounting and setting off on Glory made Cindy feel sad. So many times, *she* had dreamed of galloping him down the track. Now, even if Glory stayed permanently at Whitebrook by some miracle, Cindy herself would be gone. If anything made her want to fight to stay at Whitebrook, it was Glory. Together they had been through so much.

"I won't let them take me!" she told him. "I won't let them ruin my whole life!" But even as she contemplated running away again, Cindy knew that she couldn't do it. For so long, she had figured that she would simply take off if the authorities came to take her or Glory away. Yet in her heart, Cindy knew that Whitebrook had changed the way she acted forever. The old Cindy would have been long gone, but the new Cindy was a different person—not just in how she looked but how she behaved. If she ran away, it would just prove everything she had been trying to disprove. She would look scared of the truth—guilty. And more seriously, she would hurt the

McLeans. She had seen how they reacted when she had been missing for a few hours. She just couldn't put them through that kind of worry again. They had taught her to be responsible and sensitive to others. If she ran away, it would be like scorning everything they and Whitebrook stood for.

13

WHEN THE BUS DROPPED CINDY OFF AFTER SCHOOL ON Monday, she didn't sprint up the driveway as she usually did. Instead, she walked slowly, savoring the beauty of the afternoon. She tried to memorize exactly how everything looked so that when she was gone, she could think back on the home she had once known.

"Cindy! Cindy!" A voice broke through Cindy's sad thoughts. She glanced up and saw Samantha standing at the top of the driveway waving her arms. "Hurry up! It's about Glory!"

Forgetting about her own predicament, Cindy ran toward the house. "Please let him be safe," she prayed. "Please let him stay at Whitebrook."

Inside the house, the McLeans were gathered

around the kitchen table. "Cindy! Good news!" Beth exclaimed.

"What is it?" Cindy asked breathlessly.

Beth, Ian, and Samantha all started talking at once. It seemed that the neighbor and his son were criminals and had been caught red-handed.

"The police went over at dawn this morning to check things out," Mr. McLean explained.

"And what they found was pretty conclusive evidence," Samantha put in. "The men were in the middle of dyeing the coat of a horse to change him from a bay to a black."

Cindy sat down in a chair, stunned. "You mean you were right? The whole operation is crooked?" she asked.

"No," her foster father corrected her. "We mean *you* were right: the whole operation is crooked. We never would have known if you hadn't seen Glory being mistreated. You put us on the trail. And you protected Whitebrook by doing it. The idea of living next to somebody like that is not only repulsive, it's scary. Who's to say he wouldn't have nabbed one of our horses and then taken off for another state? We have more than a little to thank you for, Cindy."

"Boy," Cindy breathed. She sat back, flabbergasted. Beth and Samantha were congratulating her for her good thinking, but she could hardly concentrate. It seemed impossible that real live horse thieves lived next door, that she had stumbled upon such a horrible crime. She sat up with a start. "Then Glory—"

"The Jockey Club is continuing their search for his owners. We'll just have to wait and see," Ian said.

"The police found lots of evidence of what the men were up to—fake papers, tattooing equipment, you name it—but there was no record of a gray colt like Glory," Samantha explained.

"As far as I'm concerned, he has a home at Whitebrook indefinitely," Ian pronounced.

Impulsively, Cindy threw her arms around her foster father. "Thank you so much! Oh, thank you!" she cried. She had wished for this moment so often, and now it was true. For the time being, Glory could stay at Whitebrook. *At least one of us is safe*, Cindy thought.

The next morning, Ashleigh and Samantha caught Cindy at the tail end of her chores. They beeped at her from the farm Jeep. "Hey! We're driving into Lexington to go to the tack shop. Want to come?" Ashleigh called.

"Sure thing!" Cindy called, running to hop in beside the other two. Although she realized that it was probably her last outing with Samantha and

Ashleigh, she was determined not to make anyone feel sorry for her. She wasn't going to be a burden to the people who had been so good to her.

At the tack shop, Ashleigh picked up a new pair of breeches on sale, and Samantha bought a fly bonnet for Shining. "After all, we can't have her wasting her energy to get rid of the flies," she joked.

Cindy fingered a few items, fondly remembering how strange everything had once seemed. All of this—the tack, the equipment, the clothes—was part of a world that she would know no longer. She would miss every detail: even the feel of a pair of reins or a leather-backed body brush.

On the ride home, Cindy stared out the window at the acres of Kentucky pastureland. She hardly heard Ashleigh ask if she or Samantha minded if they made a brief stop at Townsend Acres. She wanted to check up on Townsend Princess and it was on the way. Immediately Cindy stiffened.

"Cindy, I know how you feel. Listen, we'll avoid Lavinia. In fact, I'll make it a really quick stop, and you can wait in the car if you want," Ashleigh said.

Cindy agreed reluctantly. She knew once she got there, she wouldn't be able to wait in the car. She'd want to get out and see Princess and the other horses, but she couldn't exactly tell Ashleigh not to stop.

When the three of them arrived at the training

area of Townsend Acres, a few of the horses were still being exercised. Cindy got out of the Jeep slowly, looking about cautiously. She felt herself trembling and knew that if she saw Lavinia, she would react violently. The woman had done everything she could to ruin Cindy's life at Whitebrook, and she had succeeded. Cindy wanted to avoid involving Samantha and Ashleigh in an ugly scene at all costs. They would jump to her defense, but it would be completely useless: her fate was sealed.

As she closed the Jeep door, she heard Ken Maddock's voice ring out angrily. "That colt is too green for you, Lavinia! Don't say I didn't warn you! I'm telling you: she's too much for you to handle." Cindy watched the trainer turn away in disgust. Lavinia was headed toward the track aboard one of the farm's young colts. Cindy froze for a second, her eyes on the pair. Luckily, Lavinia was too busy managing her spirited mount to notice Cindy's arrival.

Ashleigh and Samantha had caught sight of Hank. The old groom was leaning on the rail of the training oval, and they went to talk with him. Cindy hung back under a clump of trees. She could see that Lavinia had choked up much too far on the reins. Instead of steadying the colt with her hands, seat, and legs, she was trying to hold him at a canter by hauling repeatedly on his mouth. The colt was obviously annoyed.

Cindy glanced down the track. As always, she was thrilled by the busy, horsey scene. Suddenly she heard the unmistakable sound of thundering hooves. She turned, expecting to see one of the race horses breeze by. But it was Lavinia's horse. He had bolted, taking off with the bit between his teeth. The colt galloped wildly down the stretch. Cindy could see that Lavinia had lost her stirrups. She clutched madly at the reins as her only hope of staying on and stopping the runaway. Cindy saw the panic on Lavinia's face as her mount galloped headlong toward the rail. With an almighty heave, he jumped, trying to clear the fence. But he was going much too fast to judge the distance. His forelegs caught on the top rail. Horse and rider somersaulted through the air. Lavinia was thrown off violently. She landed in a heap, helpless as the horse fell almost on top of her.

Cindy ran as fast as she could toward the fallen pair. Her only thought was that she was the closest person to them. She raced to Lavinia's side. The horse was still down. He was thrashing around wildly in his panic, his hooves flying dangerously close to Lavinia. In another minute, he would roll over and crush her or stand up and trample her. With a tremendous lunge, Cindy grabbed the horse's bridle and urged him to his feet. Once he was up, she pulled him out of the way. Lavinia lay crumpled on the ground, not moving.

By the time the others reached them, Cindy had the horse more or less calmed down and was kneeling at Lavinia's side. "She's unconscious!" Cindy cried.

Brad rushed up, white-faced. "My God," he gasped, kneeling beside Cindy. He seized his wife's hand. "Oh, Lav—Somebody call an ambulance!" He threw his arms around his wife.

"Hank is calling," Ken Maddock said, putting a calming hand on Brad's shoulder. "Don't move her, Brad. You'll only make it worse."

It seemed to take an eternity for the ambulance to arrive. Lavinia still hadn't regained consciousness when the sirens blared in the driveway. Already a bruised contusion was darkening her cheek. Brad sat beside her, unashamedly crying.

The paramedics jumped down expertly and began to examine Lavinia. Everyone stood back to give them room except for Brad who continued to hold her hand tightly. Minutes later they had Lavinia strapped to a board and were lifting her into the ambulance. Before the doors were closed, Lavinia's eyes fluttered open for an instant. Then she lost consciousness again. Brad jumped into the ambulance to ride with his wife to the hospital. While the medical technicians secured Lavinia, he consulted with one of the paramedics.

"She's broken her arm, and they think there may be head injuries," Brad announced to the others. He paused, his eyes searching the group. They rested on Cindy. "You stopped the horse from trampling her. It—she might have been killed if you hadn't," he added hoarsely.

The ambulance sped away. For several moments, the others stood standing in a stunned group. Cindy, Ashleigh, and Samantha looked at one another, not knowing what to say or do. They truly disliked Lavinia, but it made them sick all the same to see how terrible she looked as she was loaded into the ambulance.

Ken Maddock broke the silence. "That was incredibly quick thinking," he told Cindy solemnly. "Lavinia just might owe you her life."

Cindy stared at the trainer numbly. She couldn't help thinking that she had saved the life of the person who had ruined hers.

Later that day, the phone rang in the office at Whitebrook. Nobody had been able to get much done around the farm, shocked as they were about the accident, so they were all gathered in the small room. The mood around the barn was strange. They all had reason to dislike Lavinia, but Ashleigh had made an announcement saying that, despite Whitebrook's up-and-down relations with Townsend Acres, she was sure that everyone would hope for Lavinia's quick recovery.

Ken Maddock was on the other end of the line with an update from the hospital. Ashleigh listened carefully and then hung up. "Lavinia has a broken arm, multiple bruises, and a possible concussion, but she's going to be okay," she reported. Then she added more quietly, "She may lose the baby she's carrying, though."

A buzz went through the room. "She's pregnant?" Samantha asked.

Ashleigh nodded. "During the examination, they discovered that she is about a month pregnant."

"Did she know?" Samantha asked.

"According to Ken Maddock, if she did know, she didn't tell Brad. It came as a total surprise to him," Ashleigh said.

As the others began to chatter, Cindy crept quietly away to Glory's stall. She couldn't face anyone else congratulating her for saving Lavinia. The news of the baby had thrown her thoughts into even more turmoil. She just wanted to be alone.

14

SUNDAY PASSED IN A DAZE FOR CINDY. SHE HELPED OUT IN the barn, but it felt like she was just going through the motions. She couldn't throw herself into things like before. She kept one ear cocked for the telephone at all times.

By mid-morning, the call came in from Townsend Acres. Lavinia had regained consciousness. "And the baby?" Mr. McLean inquired.

"The baby's going to be all right, too," Mike said. "And Cindy, Brad wanted me to thank you for him again. His wife owes her health—not to mention the baby's—to you and you alone. That would have been a very different phone call if you hadn't gotten that horse away from Lavinia."

Cindy smiled wanly at Mike's praise. The one

thing she could think of to say, she couldn't say. Still, she thought it, over and over: Lavinia's fine, but what about me?

"Hey, Cin, why don't we go up to the house and tell Beth?" Samantha suggested.

"Yeah, and then maybe we could give you that jumping lesson I promised," Tor added.

Cindy was only too eager to follow them out of the barn. She felt uncomfortable and awkward. But up at the house, things were no better. Beth was sitting on the couch, her face ashen. Cindy didn't have to ask what had happened. Her only question was, "When?"

"They're coming to pick you up tomorrow," Beth whispered. "It's a family over in Louisville that takes in p-problem children."

Cindy noticed Samantha and Tor exchanging glances. They turned to Cindy, trying to console her, but she shook her head. "I've known this was coming. I'll—I'll be okay," she said, her voice threatening to crack.

"Hey, why all the long faces?" Mr. McLean asked, coming through the kitchen door. "I just heard the news about Lavinia."

"Mrs. Lovell called, dear," Beth said gently, trying to soften her words. "The Child Protection Agency has found a new place for Cindy. They're coming to pick her up tomorrow. It's all settled."

Mr. McLean stopped dead, a horrified expression on his face. But instead of accepting the news quietly, he began to shout. "I'm talking to Brad!" he stormed. "I don't care if Lavinia is in the hospital, she has got to drop her accusations against Cindy! Cindy just saved her life! The only reason she's being moved is that the Townsends have convinced the state that she's a juvenile delinquent. I'm going to drive over to Lexington Memorial this instant."

His hands clenched, Mr. McLean strode off. Everyone was silent for a moment. Then Cindy spoke. In a low, trembling voice, she said, "I didn't take the watch. I swear I didn't."

"We believe you," Samantha said.

"And we always have," Tor added.

"But that doesn't do any good!" Cindy cried, finally breaking into sobs. "They're still taking me away!" Cindy jumped up, glanced wildly around the room, and ran out the door. Too late, she realized there was nowhere to run to. She couldn't face going back to the stables with everyone there.

She could dimly hear Samantha and Tor following her, calling her to stop, but she ignored them and started running again, blindly, not caring where she went. She ran smack into Mike Reese who was coming out of his house.

"Cindy! I've been—"

Cindy didn't want to hear. She didn't want to listen to anyone anymore. Fighting like a cat, she struggled to get free, but Mike put his arms around her and held her tightly until she calmed down. Samantha and Tor came running up, followed by Beth.

"Listen to me, Cindy," Mike said firmly. "I just got a call from Townsend Acres—from Hank. The grooms were cleaning out the tack boxes this morning, and guess what they found? Lavinia's blasted watch! It had fallen down inside the box."

For a minute they all stared open-mouthed at Mike. Then everyone turned and stared at Cindy. Mike let her go. Her arms dropped to her sides. She looked from Samantha to Tor to Beth to Mike. Then she tilted her head back and let out a whoop of joy so loud it spooked the horses in a nearby field. Before she could whoop again, the others had enveloped her in a huge bear hug.

"Wait a minute! Dad's on his way to the hospital. I've got to try and reach him before he finds Brad!" Samantha cried. She disentangled herself and ran toward the house.

"Come on, let's go with her," Beth said through her tears. She put a motherly arm around Cindy. "I think we could all use a cup of tea."

*   *   *

181

"So what kind of cake do you want?" Samantha asked Cindy. Although darkness had fallen, a group was lingering in the training barn. Tor was leaning against a stall door and Heather stood next to him. The McLeans were busy in the office, tying up some business. The past week had flown by in a series of calls to and from the hospital, Townsend Acres, and Child Protection Services. As soon as the Townsends had dropped the charges, the state authorities had told Mrs. Lovell that there was no justified reason for forcing Cindy to make a traumatic move to a different family.

"Carrot cake, of course," Tor joked. "So she can give some to Glory."

"That's right—don't forget this party is as much a celebration for him as it is for me," Cindy said judiciously.

"Can you manage a carrot cake, Beth?" Samantha asked, as her stepmother joined them.

"Oh, I think maybe just this once," Beth replied, her eyes twinkling. Mr. McLean emerged from the office after her and put an arm around his wife.

"I think we should have games, too," he said. "How about 'Pin the Tail on Glory'?"

"More like 'Pin the Tattoo Identification Number,' Dad," Samantha said kiddingly.

"I would say that we could play 'Name the twin

orphan foals,'" Cindy said, "but I've already done that."

"What? You mean you thought up names for them?" Samantha asked excitedly.

Cindy nodded shyly. "I kept thinking about how if it weren't for how gentle they looked, I would never have risked sleeping in the stable that first night. Those foals brought me good luck, and now things look even better. I thought we could call one Four Leaf Clover and one Rainbow."

"Clover and Rainbow!" Samantha exclaimed. "They're perfect!"

"Knock-knock, can we join you?"

The small group looked up to see Ashleigh and Mike entering the barn. "The more the merrier," Samantha said. "Come help plan the party."

"We just had to come say how happy we are that you're going to stay with the McLeans, Cindy," Mike said, smiling fondly at her. "They're lucky to have you as a foster child."

"I'm sorry to tell you, Mike, that I'm not exactly their foster child anymore," Cindy said in mock gravity.

Mike raised an eyebrow in surprise. "What do you mean?"

"Well, as soon as the adoption papers come through, I'm going to be the McLeans' real child," Cindy said with a shy grin.

"That's right—and you'll be my real sister," Samantha put in. "I've always wanted a sister."

Cindy gave her a radiant smile. Then she reached up to stroke Glory who was standing beside her in the aisle. Now that Cindy was going to have a real identity and real parents, they were no closer to finding out Glory's true identity.

"I hope they never find your owner," Cindy whispered to him softly.

Glory whickered softly in reply. If only the two of them could stay at Whitebrook together forever.

Joanna Campbell was born and raised in Norwalk, Connecticut and grew up loving horses. She eventually owned a horse of her own and took riding lessons for a number of years, specializing in jumping. She still rides when possible and has started her three-year-old granddaughter on lessons. In addition to publishing over twenty-five novels for young adults, she is the author of four adult novels. She has also sung and played piano professionally and owned an antique business. She now lives on the coast of Maine in Camden with her husband, Ian Bruce. She has two children, Kimberly and Kenneth, and three grandchildren.